I Get a Clue

—from My Edinburgh Files

I Get a Clue

—from *My Edinburgh Files*

Nancy Ellen Hird

Desert Fires Press

I Get a Clue
—from My Edinburgh Files

ISBN: 978-0-9858923-0-2

Published by Desert Fires Press

Cover illustration: Jenna Freck

Edinburgh cover photo: Sigrid Nielsen

Book Website: www.desertfirespress.com

E-mail: desertfirespress@yahoo.com

Printed in U.S.A

For all the young girls standing on the threshold
of womanhood and wondering
about the next step

The Lord is my shepherd; I shall not want.
He maketh me to lie down in green pastures:
he leadeth me beside still waters.
He restoreth my soul:
he leadeth me in the paths of righteousness
for his name's sake.

PSALM 23:1-3

CHAPTER 1

Horrible Night in July—9:46 PM

My heart pounding, I stood up. "I'm not going," I said to my parents. "You can't do this to me. I'm not going to Scotland. And I'm not going to Quito. I'm staying right here." Head high, I exited my dad's study. In my room I made a sign and taped it to my door—I'm Not Moving!

I shut the door and leaned against it. Only thirty minutes before, my life had been kind of terrific. And now—and now, it was hurtling toward a black hole. How could this be happening?

Terrific Night Only 30 Minutes Before

I licked more of the warm goo off of my fingers—peach pie floating in a lake of melting vanilla ice cream. Yum! Life was good—my mom's pie, my telescope waiting for

1

me on the patio, and Krissy's pool party tomorrow. Yes, things were good. I turned to put the ice cream carton away and saw my dad standing in the kitchen doorway. He was looking at me curiously. He tapped his fingers on the door frame.

"Elizabeth, Mom and I need to see you in my study."

"I didn't do anything wrong," I protested as I closed the freezer.

"Nobody said you did."

"You called me 'Elizabeth.' You never call me 'Elizabeth' except when I'm in trouble."

"No, I don't. Do I?" Dad pushed his round-rimmed glasses back up his nose. "I'm sorry. Well, you're not in trouble." He peered at me like a blond owl and then grinned. "Unless there's something I don't know about."

I did a virus check over my day. I grinned back. "There's not."

"OK, in my study, Libby."

"Do you want some pie, Dad?" I set my plate on the counter and turned away to cut a piece of pie for him.

"Sounds good, but later," he said.

I don't know if he ate any pie later. All I know was I should have eaten mine at that very moment. I would have enjoyed it.

I carried my plate and followed Dad. That was not easy. Boxes—packing boxes—littered our living room and hall. Some boxes were marked for storage. Others marked for Quito, Ecuador. We were moving. In just a few weeks Quito was going to be our new home.

Dad and I navigated the sea of boxes expertly. Upstairs Mags stopped doing scales on her cello and began playing the Saint-Saens. For a moment Dad and I stood in the hallway and just listened. Too beautiful. (At seventeen my sister is an awesome cellist. She's going to be famous someday. I know it.)

"You've got it, honey," Dad called up to her. He smiled and then his face turned sad. I felt sad too. It had hit me, like it probably had hit him, how much we were going to miss hearing Mags play.

You see, when I said "our" new home, I meant the parents and me. My brother and sister weren't going with us. Tom was going to college and Mags was staying in California with her best friend and her family. Senior year and all that stuff.

Truthfully, when the parents had dropped the news a year earlier that they were praying about going to the mission field, I asked my Sunday school class every week to pray that God would say no. Huge disappointment. God didn't say, "No." Six months later my dad, the computer genius, was signed up to work for Los Mensajeros—in Quito, Ecuador.

I freaked. I was mad, but I "adjusted." (As my mother put it.) It was going to be fun, an adventure.

When Dad and I got to his study, Mom was sitting on the couch. She patted the leather cushion beside her and I sat down. Casually Dad seated himself on the edge of his desk. He started tapping his fingers on its wooden top. I glanced at Mom. She was chewing her cheek. I took a bite of pie, but hardly tasted it. Maybe I wasn't in trouble, but something was up. Mom smiled at Dad, cueing him I thought.

"Libby, Mom and I have been praying about this move and we've decided that you should not come to Ecuador with us."

My mind cartwheeled. Was I going to stay with Krissy? Her parents had offered and—wow—that would be great! Of course, I would miss the parents but wow, I wouldn't have to change schools or leave my friends or try to get along in a foreign language. This was going to—

"Mom has been talking to Gran and Aunt Susannah, and we've decided that you should live with them in Edinburgh."

"Scotland?" I could barely get the word out. "Decided? But why? Why do I have to go there? Why can't I go with you?" I felt panicky. "This isn't fair. Why didn't you talk to me first?"

They said a lot of stuff about Gran needing help with the B&B (bed-and-breakfast), and my being safer there, and the chance to learn more about my roots. (My mother is from Scotland.) They also threw in the Royal Observatory (like the Royal Observatory is going to invite some 11-nearly-12-year-old kid to look through their telescope. Right!!!)

I was not buying any of it, but I knew better than to weep and wail. I had watched Mags too many times. Calmly, I handed my mother my plate of unfinished pie, excused myself and went to my room.

There I made a list of ten sound reasons why I should go to Ecuador and why I shouldn't be exiled to Edinburgh. I then returned to the study and presented my list to the parents. The way I saw it, they had only two reasons—Mom wanted it and Dad wanted it. My home, it turned out, is the only place in the whole world where two is more than ten.

My life was way out of my control—traveling at warp speed into a black hole. I had to try to stop it. I made the sign and stuck it on the door. Scotland and I just weren't going to be a possibility.

CHAPTER 2

Same Unbelievably Awful Night

After taping up my sign, I shut the door firmly. (I get in big trouble when I slam.) I punched Play on the CD player on my desk and threw myself on the bed. I tried to lose myself in the music. I tried hard not to think about anything. I tried hard not to cry. It didn't work. I cried.

I was on my second CD when there was a knock at the door. Tom poked his head into the room. "Hey, *enfant.*" (*Enfant* is French for baby. Mags started calling me that a couple of years ago. She thought it was cute. I didn't mind then, but lately I minded. I minded a lot.)

"I'm not a baby and you're not supposed to call me that anymore," I said sourly.

Tom put his hands up in surrender. "Sorry. Can I come in?"

I shrugged. "I don't know, CAN you?"

He strolled across the room and dropped into my desk chair. Putting his hands behind his head, he stretched his long legs out into the room. My brother is tall and looks skinny, though he's got plenty of muscles. I call him Tommy Tree when I'm not mad at him. I sometimes call him Tommy Tree in front of his girlfriends just to make him turn red.

"Cool sign," he said, nodding toward the door. "Yellow out-lined with black. Very effective."

"I'm glad you like it," I said and pulled at a loose thread on my quilt. "Won't do any good, though."

"Nope, afraid not."

"It's not fair. Why do I have to go to Edinburgh?"

"Because ..." He frowned. "Things don't seem fair sometimes. That's life. You make plans, you pack your car, you get to the campground and it's full. You don't always get what you want."

"But why not? If it's a good something, why shouldn't you get it?"

"I don't know. It's kind of a mystery, I guess." He ran a hand through his brown hair and stared at the ceiling. "Right now I'm just hoping it's because God has something better planned," he said softly, more to himself than to me.

Some of my anger slid away. Tom hadn't been accepted to Stanford and he had wanted to go badly. The day the rejection letter came I had seen my big brother, who didn't cry even when Krissy's dog bit him, reading that letter with his face all twisted up. I had cried.

But two weeks later Tom got accepted to UC Davis, and he decided to go there.

"I'll tell you what," he said, smiling. "We'll make a pact. I'll watch for the cool stuff that God does where I am and e-mail you. You watch for what He does in Edinburgh and e-mail me."

I frowned. "Do I have to be happy about all this?"

"No."

"Good, because I'm not."

"Do we have a deal, Lillibet?"

"But nothing great is going to happen in Edinburgh. So I'll have nothing to write."

Tom shrugged. "Do we have a deal?"

I rolled my eyes and I sighed. "I guess."

CHAPTER 3

Tuesday Morning, Three Weeks Later

M ags slept on the plane. (I told my mother I didn't need anyone to go WITH. She said Mags would go WITH for two weeks and have a holiday—end of discussion.)

I didn't sleep on the plane. Not a nanosecond. I was still mad about being sent to Scotland and, truthfully, a little scared. Sure I closed my eyes on the long—fourteen hours, fifty-three minutes long—flight as I flew away from my family, my home and my friends. But I didn't sleep. And when my sister took a lock of her red hair and tickled my cheek, I felt it immediately.

"Come on, Mags, I'm not a baby anymore." I pushed her hand away.

Mags grinned and stretched her arms over her head—plane seats being way confining. I stretched too but knocked the pillow of the woman sitting next to me. It landed on the floor. And then trying to pick it up for her, I stepped on the pillow.

Someday, I'm going to have my sister's poise, sophistication and *savoir faire*. Not in the near future, but someday. I've totally given up on ever having her looks. Mags is pretty, super pretty. Oh, not California surfer girl pretty, all tan and stuff. My sister is pretty like a storybook princess.

She sighed dramatically and fluttered her long lashes. "You're such a grump. And if you don't stop, I'm going to—" Her green eyes lit up. She had looked just like that yesterday when we put cornflakes in Tom's bed. (Just to give him something to remember us.)

"OK. OK. How's this?" I pushed the corners of my mouth into a smile with my fingers.

"Good. Now stop slouching. Sit up. The flight attendant is nearly here with our breakfast. Remember we are women of the world. We have flyer miles."

I giggled and let down my tray.

Mags unlatched hers. Then she unbuckled the dog wristwatch from her arm and dangled it in front of me. "Here, we need to trade back."

"No, not yet." I covered the gold watch on my wrist protectively with my hand. I love my dog watch. The dog has the funniest face and its front paws point to the numbers. But I really, really wanted to keep wearing the gold one. It's my mom's. "I think Mom should have let me take care of her watch for her instead of you," I complained.

Mags shook her head. "You would lose it, *enfant*."

Again with that word. I wasn't a baby. When were they going to stop calling me that?! And when were they going to stop treating me like one?!

"Give." Mags thrust her open palm at me. Frowning, I unbuckled Mom's watch and gave it to my sister.

When we landed at Glasgow, the sky was gray and sloshing down rain. "A perfect summer day. I thought this was August," I muttered, reaching under the seat for my backpack.

"Sh-h-h," Mags said. Her head jerked toward the blue uniformed woman beside her—our flight attendant, Jodie.

"Girls, I'll help you get through immigration. Then we need to get your luggage and go through customs. We'll wait for your aunt at the reservations counter." She smiled brightly and smoothed her short blond hair behind her ears.

Mags has this ability to make friends anywhere, anytime. She and Jodie were best buds by the time we got through customs. Anything you'd like to know about life as a flight attendant? Just ask Mags. She's got all the info.

We waited at the reservations counter fifteen minutes. Jodie and Mags talked clothes. I sat on my suitcase, staring at the floor. Jodie and Mags talked music. I stared at the crowds. Another fifteen minutes passed.

"What does Aunt Susannah look like," I interrupted.

"You met her," Mags said.

"I was little. I don't remember."

"You saw her picture."

"The one that was taken years ago?" I protested.

"She's pretty and has dark hair like Mom, but she's a little shorter. More my height."

I scanned the women coming and going. "That describes a lot of them. Are you sure you'll recognize her?"

"Well, it seems to me Mom asked her to make it easy for us to spot her. She's going to wear full Highland dress—kilt in the Stewart plaid, of course, knee socks, and a white ruffled blouse."

"You're kidding, right?"

"I'm kidding."

I sure hoped so. Looking around the room, the women I saw were wearing summer dresses or pants and jackets.

Jodie glanced at her watch. "I'm going to check. Probably there's a message for you." She walked behind the counter and picked up a phone.

"Maybe," I said, "Aunt Susannah walked right past us. And now she's decided we missed the plane. Wished we had missed the plane. She's probably left, gone home. Maybe we should call Mom."

"Not yet. Besides, for Mom it's still the middle of the night."

Jodie returned. Her smile seemed a little forced. "Your aunt's been delayed. There are some restaurants, cafeteria-style, upstairs. We'll leave the luggage behind the counter and get some coffee. You're going to love the pastries here. The haggis I would avoid. But the pastries—they're scrumptious."

"What's haggis?" I whispered to Mags as we followed Jodie.

"Sheep's stomach and other meat—cooked."

"Ugh! Do people eat it a lot?"

"It's the national dish," Mags said matter-of-factly.

The cafeteria was at the far end of this huge, gymnasium-size room. I wasn't hungry so I filled a big cup with orange soda, found a straw, and dragged myself to a table. (My Reeboks had turned into concrete during the flight.) Jodie and Mags took seats and dove into gooey, chocolatey pastries. Over each bite they exclaimed and then worried about the calories. I sipped my drink and closed my eyes. I was falling, falling ...

Suddenly I jerked upright. Right away I noticed something was different. Mags and Jodie had stopped talking. I opened my eyes. They were gone. I swiveled around in my chair and scanned the food counters. I whipped my head to the lounge area that made up the rest of the room. Mags and Jodie weren't there either. They weren't anywhere. Swallowing the growing knot in my throat, I stood up. My knees wobbled.

"I drink too much coffee," Jodie said, coming up behind me. She was carrying a paper cup.

I sat down, burying my face in my soda cup, and hoped she hadn't seen my panic. I glanced up and forced a smile. If she had seen my fear, I hoped she wouldn't say anything to Mags when she came back.

But Mags didn't come. At least five minutes passed. I checked "the dog." "Where is Mags?" I asked.

"She went to the loo—the ladies' room." Jodie pointed over her shoulder.

At the far end of the room was a sign for the restroom. Jodie eyed me closely, then she said gently. "You fell asleep. She hasn't been gone long. It just seems that way."

I nodded. Another five minutes passed. I started watching the restroom door. Another five minutes passed. Why was Mags taking so long? I halfway stood, my eyes darting around the room.

"I need to—" I pointed to the restroom. Jodie nodded and I ran. Breathing hard, I shoved the door open. "Mags?" I called, two decibels below a scream. She wasn't at the sink. The two stalls were occupied and I quickly bent down. One pair of feet wore black heels. The other set of feet wore cute, camel-colored flats just like Mags, but the feet were large—too large to be my sister's. My throat tightened and I shivered, but not from cold. I turned, ripped open the door and streaked across the lounge. Jodie was still sitting alone at the table. And at a time like this she was engrossed in a book!!!

"She's—she's not there!" I yelped, tears smarting my eyes and about to explode down my face.

Jodie—I couldn't believe it—went into a trance. She stared beyond me at the restroom. Except for twisting her earring, she didn't move.

"Police!" I exclaimed, wanting to shake her. "We have to call the police. Something, somebody has—" I couldn't finish. I broke down and sobbed. I was miles from my family, in a foreign country, and now my sister was missing, and nobody would help me find her.

Jodie stood up. "I'm sure she's all right," she said, patting my shoulder, but I noticed that her eyes scanned the crowds. Suddenly she stiffened and pursed her lips. "She probably just decided to go into one of the shops across the way. You were asleep and I was getting coffee so, of course, she wouldn't have said anything."

I shook my head and sniffled. "She wouldn't just leave— She's supposed to take care of me. I know she wouldn't just—"

"Let's pick up our things and find a courtesy phone. I know where there is one downstairs," Jodie said firmly, calmly. "We'll have her paged." She put the book in her purse and led the way to the escalator.

I tried swiping the tears off my cheeks, but they came faster than I could swipe. People were staring at me—I was sure of it. Humiliated, I followed Jodie, my eyes on the floor.

"Look, Libby, there," Jodie said.

I swung my head to where she was pointing. Stepping onto the escalator on the floor below was Mags.

"Mags!" I screeched.

Mags gave me that I-love-you-too-but-what's-all-the-excitement-about look. I jumped on the escalator and took the steps as fast as I could. At the bottom I threw my arms around my sister and hugged her tight.

Mags hugged me. "OK, Libby, OK, but what's wrong?"

"She became a little concerned when you didn't return right away," Jodie explained.

Mags shook her head. "The ladies' upstairs was full and with a line. I went to the one downstairs. But that one was being cleaned. I had to wait. Then I did my makeup and brushed my teeth. I wasn't gone all that long, was I? Libby, did you think I'd been kidnapped? You did. Oh, Libby, if someone tried to snatch me, you would have heard it. Everyone would have. I would have screamed and yelled."

I felt like an idiot. I felt like a baby.

"Margaret." A woman called and waved from across the room.

Mags turned and waved back. "Aunt Susannah," she whispered to me. The smiling woman coming toward us wore a stylish khaki raincoat over jeans. No plaid— anywhere. She was pretty like Mags, but her short hair was dark like my mom's. It bounced as she walked.

"Margaret," Aunt Susannah said, throwing her arms around Mags. I waited for Mags to correct her. She didn't. "We're so glad you've come. Your grandmother has already chosen two concerts for you to attend. And Elizabeth," she said, hugging me. "We're going to have such fun. I was thinkin' I've not seen you since you were shorter than the fairies." She stepped back and looked at me. "You're a young lady now and tall. I think you're fair taller than your sister. And me."

I shrunk down. At five feet five inches, I was all too aware that I was becoming a giant. I had grown three inches since Easter.

"Thank you for looking after them. Sorry to be delayed," Aunt Susannah said to Jodie. "I had to take the bus. The lorry had a breakdown."

"Laurie who?" I asked.

"Not Laurie. L-o-r-r-y," Mags corrected. "It's a truck."

"Oh, great," I muttered to myself, "they don't speak English here."

"Truth be said, Mr. MacLeod's vehicle is a van," Aunt Susannah said. "Mr. MacLeod owns the bakery on Bruntsfield and he offered himself and his delivery van to us. It worked fine yesterday. But today the beastly thing no would start. Pity because the van would have been a grand help with the luggage." She looked about questioningly. "Now this is travelin' light."

"Our bags are at the reservation desk," Margaret (Mags) said, leading the way.

"Elizabeth, I suspect you brought everything you own," teased Aunt Susannah.

"Mom said she will ship the rest of Libby's school clothes next week," Margaret (Mags) said.

Aunt Susannah shook her head. "We'll ring your mother tonight. She need not send many clothes. Tomorrow, Elizabeth, I'll take you to Princes Street and we'll shop for your school uniform." She grabbed the handle of my suitcase. "Come, we need to be quick. We no want to miss our bus."

"What?" I didn't move. "Uniform? I'm not wearing—"

CHAPTER 4

First Afternoon in Edinburgh

From: Libby Carlsen
Subject: nothing
To: Tom Carlsen <carlsenT@christiancom.net>

Dear Tom,

Nothing. Nothing has happened!! Oh, we had to take the bus and a cab because the lorry (not L-a-u-r-i-e) broke down. And now we're here.

i have to get off. Mags is standing over me like a flapping goose. She has to EM her 100 friends. i'll bet she already has 40 messages in her inbox. i didn't have one. :(

Libby

That's the first e-mail I sent to my brother on the day Mags and I arrived. I still can't believe that's all I wrote.

(Forget that Mags was practically pulling me out of the chair. She didn't bother me that much.) I was, I guess, having a sulk, as my mother would say. I didn't want to admit to my brother that I had seen and heard "things." Even though I HAD seen and heard "things."

CHAPTER 5

Earlier That Day (Tuesday)

Before I came to Edinburgh, my idea of a B&B was a Victorian mansion with turrets and porches and lots of garden. I pictured Gran's house as being in the country someplace. Not in the middle of a big city. When Aunt Susannah said Shepherd House was at the end of the street that our taxi had just turned onto, I couldn't believe it. I stared out of the window. Skinny three-story houses filled one side of the block. They stood right up next to each other, shoulder to shoulder like soldiers.

"Redcoats," I said to myself, as our cab inched its way up the narrow street. Redcoats like in the Revolutionary War. Americans, beware. Any moment the command will be given. "Load. Aim. Fire!"

I checked out the tall trees on the opposite side of the street. Their trunks were wide. They would hide me if I ducked behind one of them. Only problem was the taller-than-Goliath stone wall smack up against those tree trunks. I was trapped. Nowhere to run. Nowhere to hide.

I slumped in the seat and glared at the houses.

What were my parents thinking? How could they send me here? Where were the basketball hoops over the garages? Where were the friendly green lawns running down to the sidewalk?

Even the flowers looked pathetic. They were in teeny, tiny gardens, cut off from the street by waist-high stone walls. Prisoners, I decided. The flowers were prisoners, like me.

The taxi came to a stop at the end of the block, and Aunt Susannah smiled at me. I jerked up to get a better look. In front of us was a parking lot. I stared. The big house off to my right, Gran's house, didn't even have a garden.

The black asphalt parking lot was empty except for a white delivery van off to the side. A blond kid who was about my age was standing beside the van. He handed a wrench to someone underneath it. A sign in blue lettering on the van said "MacLeod's." I noticed the boy looked worried, and for a couple of moments I wondered why. Then I got out of the taxi and put one heavy foot in front of the other. I had my own problems.

Aunt Susannah and Mags led the way up the front steps. I trudged behind, lugging my big black duffel bag. As I crossed into the entry hall, a woman in a hurry bumped into me. I lost my balance and stupidly tripped over the suitcase Mags was pulling. The next thing I knew I was up close and personal with the tiles of Gran's mosaic floor.

"No! No!" I cried, sitting up and grabbing my duffel. I unzipped it and tore at the clothes wrapped around a long black case.

"I'm sure it's OK," Mags said. "I'm sure nothing is broken." She touched my shoulder reassuringly.

"*Que lastima!*" exclaimed the woman who had bumped into me. "You are hurt, *si?*"

I shook my head. "It's my—"

She ignored me and turned to Gran, who had come rushing into the entry hall and now stood over me. "Senora Stewart, I am not clumsy." She tossed her long black ponytail back across her shoulders. Amazingly, her hair reached almost to her waist. "But accidents, they happen, no?" she said. "*Hay lo siento.* Very sorry. I still have my job, *si?*"

"Yes, of course, Alejandra. Of course," Gran said. "Come again tomorrow at ten."

"*Gracias,*" she said and left, her hair swinging across her back, her sandals slapping the tile floor.

Mags squatted and helped me pull out the case. I unsnapped the locks.

"Dear, what is it?" Gran asked.

"It's her telescope," Mags said softly.

"Oh, no," Gran said, coming and kneeling beside me. She ran a hand along the tube of the telescope, then touched the case. "It's a sturdy case. If I know your father, it is sure that he packed this so that a drop from a second floor window would no injure it." She smiled. "You'll assemble it and you'll see."

I swallowed hard and nodded.

Behind me heavy steps sounded on the front steps.

"Miss Stewart, a wee word with you, if I may," said a man. His voice was deep like a string bass and his words sounded almost like singing. I looked over my shoulder. The man almost filled the doorway. Muscles bulged from his grease stained T-shirt.

"Surely, Mr. MacLeod," Aunt Susannah said happily. "Mr. MacLeod, these are my nieces from America, Margaret and Elizabeth. Girls, this is Mr. MacLeod. He owns the bakery on Bruntsfield."

"It's a pleasure to meet you both," he said. "I apologize for my van. Its breakdown caused you some inconvenience to be sure." He ran a large hand across his shaven head. "Vans, they sometimes have minds of their own." He winked. Then with his head he gestured for Aunt Susannah to join him in the entry hall.

"Well, my girls," Gran said, "it is past time for you to have settled in. Yours is a lovely room at the top of the staircase, number ten." She walked toward the steps and put her hand on the mahogany post. She stopped. "But we mayn't go up just yet. I have no given my girls a kiss. Nor have I received one." Going to Mags, she kissed her on the cheek and hugged her tight. Then she turned to me and opened her arms. "Elizabeth, we are so glad to have you."

I scrambled to my feet. "Oh, Gran," I said, burying my head in her shoulder. Surprising myself, I burst into tears.

"Really, Libby, what's wrong with you?" Mags said.

"Sh-h, Margaret. She's had a long journey and she's been through many changes. It's no surprise she's unsettled." Gran patted me on the back.

Then she brought out a tissue from the pocket of her sweater and dabbed my cheeks. "Elizabeth, you're a fine, brave girl to come all this way. And you're goin' to get on here wonderfully. You'll see. You've got the jet lag now. Horrid thing it is. You need a wee nap and a proper meal. That will set a lot right." She hugged me again, then picking up one of the suitcases led the way up the stairs. Mags followed. I sniffled my way to my duffel bag and telescope. Squatting down, I locked the telescope case and began shoving clothes into the bag.

"Aye, Susannah, it is troublin'." I overheard Mr. MacLeod say. "A question, if you will. Did you notice anyone other than a guest in the car park last evening?"

"No, I can't say that I did," she said. "But I had no need to come to this part of the house. We had no late arriving guests."

"Would you ask your mother if she noticed anyone?"

"I will. Are you thinkin', Jock, that someone could be responsible for the breakdown?"

"Libby, will you come on!" Mags shouted from the first landing.

I picked up my duffel slowly. I wanted to hear Mr. MacLeod's answer, but he must have become aware of me. He and Aunt Susannah moved down the steps. I glanced over my shoulder. They were still talking, but their voices were too low for me to hear what they were saying.

I did see their faces. Aunt Susannah looked shocked and a little scared. Mr. MacLeod shook his head, his beard wobbling. He reminded me of my dad when he was trying to solve a puzzle and something didn't make sense.

CHAPTER 6

Wednesday Morning—Way Early!!

Something was squawking. "Bird," my brain said, "but not like a bird at home. Birds at home chirp. Why wasn't this bird chirping?" I opened my eyes.

Bright light was sliding through flowered drapes. I stared at the drapes and then at the peach-colored walls beside them. This was not my room. Definitely not my room. Where was I? Oh, yeah, Scotland.

In the other bed, Mags was making "sleep noises." (If I told you she snored, she'd kill me.) I rolled over and looked at the travel clock on the night table—5:45. Mags scooted down farther under the white duvet. Clearly, the message was—do not disturb.

Trying to be quiet, I got up. Br-r-r, it was cold. Had this place ever heard of summer? I grabbed my robe from the bottom of my bed and still shivering went to the window. I peeked between the drapes.

Outside it was already day. I couldn't believe it. And sunny. Big white cottony clouds chugged across a blue, blue sky. Three seagulls swooping and landing were playing some kind of a noisy game. It was their squawking that had awakened me.

One of them flapped toward me and landed on the shingles just below my window. He eyed me and then turned to watch his two friends chase each other. I grinned. It was tag. They were playing tag. It looked like fun.

I ran a finger along the tube of my telescope. It had checked out fine the night before. Gran had been right. Nothing had broken. I pushed the drapes apart a little and pointed my telescope at the building across the street.

It was large, three-stories tall, and red brick with lots of chimneys. It kept people out (or maybe in) with the Goliath-tall wall. Last night I had asked if it were an old factory. Gran said it was my school.

I pointed the telescope at a room on the top story of the school and adjusted the sights. A blank beige wall. Boring! Next week, when I started going there, was going to be so wonderful. Not!

Frowning, I turned the scope to the building beyond the school yard. Yellow-white stone. And long, very long. The building stretched out until the view of it was blocked by a church spire. I counted the stories—five. Tall, narrow windows and tall, wider ones ran on each floor. At the street level were doors of red, green, and royal blue. Was it an office building?

I focused on a window on the fourth floor. I saw a lamp, but not an office lamp. It had a fancy shade. I sighted on another window. Oops, a girl was standing there, looking out. She was wearing pajamas.

"What are you doing?" Mags demanded.

"I—nothing, now," I said.

"I don't think that peering into other people's houses is what Mom and Dad had in mind when they bought you a telescope."

"You don't have to say that. I know—"

There was a knock on the door. The alarm on the clock beeped.

"Girls," called a voice softly from the other side of the door. It sounded like Aunt Susannah.

I unlatched the door and opened it. (The door was latched because the room was usually rented out, but Gran said the room would now be mine.)

Already dressed in a white cotton blouse and navy-blue skirt, Aunt Susannah stepped in. "Slept well I trust. Splendid. Dress quickly now, won't you? You'll want a good breakfast before we start servin' the guests. It will no be good if we are eyeing theirs with envious looks." She grinned, her eyebrows shooting up playfully.

I liked her.

"Did I explain about the shower?" she asked.

Mags nodded.

"And you understand about the electricals? You've got to put in the adaptor when you use your blow dryer."

What was she talking about? I turned to Mags. She gave me the I'll-explain-it-later look.

"Good. See you in the kitchen in a bit," Aunt Susannah said. "Elizabeth, your mother said you like porridge for breakfast, right?"

"Porridge? You mean like in 'The Three Bears?'"

"No, like in oatmeal," Mags said, rolling her eyes.

I felt like an idiot. "I like oatmeal," I mumbled.

Aunt Susannah squeezed my shoulder and smiled. "A true Scot. Thirty minutes? Good." She pulled the door closed behind her.

"It doesn't take me an hour-plus to eat. Why do we have to get up so early?"

"We have to do morning set-up." Mags threw back the duvet and hopped out of bed. "And Gran has Bible reading after we eat."

I frowned.

"It'll be OK, Libby. It's not chapters and chapters. What I don't like is that we have to wear skirts and may not wear T-shirts."

"Gran said that?"

"Yeah. Pull the drapes shut, will you?" Mags disappeared into our in-the-room bathroom.

A non-T-shirt world? It was too much to ask. I plodded to the window and reached for the drapes. I heard footsteps coming from below. Someone at this hour was in Gran's parking lot. I got as close to the window as I could, but I couldn't see anyone. What was the person doing down there? The questions Mr. MacLeod had asked Aunt Susannah the day before replayed in my mind. Did Mr. MacLeod believe the van had broken down on its own? Or did he think someone had ...? Could this person be ...? A door slammed and a man came around in front of the van; his head was shaven and he had a beard. Whew! It was Mr. MacLeod.

CHAPTER 7

Later That Morning (Wednesday)

Breakfast for the guests was served between 8:00 and 9:30 in a room on the main floor opposite the stairs. The room had been a living room when the house was a parsonage. Now it was a dining room with eight small tables. Two to four people sat at each table.

Gran said I should serve the toast and English muffins that morning. I tried to do a good job. Even though I didn't want to be in Edinburgh, I didn't want my family to think I couldn't BE in Edinburgh. You know what I mean. That I couldn't handle it. So I tried to be the world's greatest waitress.

I failed miserably. Mags got a harder job and was still so much better than me. She asked the guests whether they wanted the whole English breakfast—eggs, beans, juice, bacon, ham, tomato, or part thereof, and then kept what they said straight. I got confused about who ordered muffins and who ordered toast and whether they wanted white or wheat.

The guests were mostly nice about it. A couple from the north of England (England is not Scotland and Scotland is not England. The Scots are quite particular on that matter.) were especially kind. They ate wheat toast when they had ordered white. A man from Germany sent his back.

Feeling like the plate weighed a ton, I trudged to the kitchen. Aunt Susannah took the rejected toast and put her arm across my shoulder. "Elizabeth, don't let them knock the wheels off your cart," she said, giving me a quick squeeze.

A hard lump formed in my throat and I tried hard not to cry, but the tears got away and rolled down my cheeks.

"Did I say somethin' wrong?" she asked.

"No," I sniffled, swiping at my cheeks. "Just, my mom says that about the cart a lot."

Aunt Susannah nodded kindly. "Here," she said, handing me two plates of the complete English breakfast. Her face was full of you-can-do-this. "Take these please to table four—the American couple."

I took a deep breath and walked carefully into the breakfast room. Nothing slid off the plates. Not even the tomatoes. I felt terrific.

The Browns, the couple at table four, were from Maryland. They were great. They joked with me and then told me their daughter, who was in college, worked part-time as a waitress. They said I was getting my training early.

I laughed. As I did I glanced out the window into the parking lot. The blond kid from yesterday was also getting training. He was standing beside the van again, tools in one hand. It was strange though. Mr. Macleod had driven off in the van yesterday afternoon. It had been fixed. Did vans break down overnight?

On my way back to the kitchen Aunt Susannah stopped me. "Take these, will you? There's a good girl," she said, handing me two steaming mugs. She nodded toward the open front door. "The coffee's for Mr. MacLeod. The cocoa's for Malcolm. Perhaps they would have me fry them an egg or two. Ask them, please, will you?"

"Sure." I walked slowly, very slowly, carrying the nearly full mugs. "Please, please," I kept telling myself, "don't spill or trip." Going down Gran's front stairs, I watched my feet the whole way. I was in the parking lot before it felt safe to look up and walk normally. And that's when I took a good look at Malcolm.

He was wearing jeans and a dark green sweatshirt. Outstanding! Did the girls over here also wear jeans and sweatshirts? That would be stupendous.

Malcolm turned around, his blond hair falling in his eyes. He pushed it back with his hand. I noticed that he had a long nose and that his ears stuck out, but only a little. He was only—maybe—a half inch shorter than me. (Most of the boys at home are way shorter.) He stared at me for a moment, kind of thoughtful, then he dropped his eyes and shoved his hands into his pockets.

"Are you Malcolm?" I asked. Yes, I know. I know that was stupid, but I couldn't think of anything else to say. But

Malcolm didn't seem to mind. He just nodded. I handed him the steaming mugs. "This is for you. And this one is for Mr. MacLeod."

"Da, a cuppa for you," Malcolm said, setting the mug on the ground beside the van. He stood up and sipped his cocoa. "Thank you. Tastes fine."

I smiled. Then it was my turn to stare at the ground. My feet, I noticed, were huge even in black flats. I wrapped one foot behind my ankle. Then put it back immediately. Standing like a flamingo wasn't going to impress anyone. I chewed my lower lip. Should I tell Malcolm my name? Did he want to know?

"I'm—"

"Good morning," called a man's voice. It was Mr. Brown. His wife walked toward a blue car but he came toward us. "Bought some carrot cakes from your bakery yesterday," he said to Malcolm. "Delicious."

Malcolm stood taller. "Thank you, sir. They are a specialty of ours."

Mr. Brown grinned. "Well, I plan to sample more of your specialties." He cocked his head. "Problems with the van again today?"

Malcolm looked uneasy. "M'dad is seein' to it."

Mr. MacLeod slid out from the van. His chin was set and his eyes angry. "I don't see how that could have come loose of its own," he muttered. He took a sip from the mug and stared at Mr. Brown. "Oh," he said, putting down the mug and jumping to his feet. He wiped his hand on his shirt and then offered it. "It's Mr. Brown, is it, no?"

The two men shook hands.

"Yes, I was going to phone today and ask to visit your facilities. Beginning of next week, all right?"

Visit a bakery? I stared at Mr. Brown. Wasn't he just a tourist? Apparently not.

"Anytime, Mr. Brown, anytime," Mr. MacLeod said.

"Monday about two o'clock."

The gate clanged behind us. "*Buongiorno! Buongiorno!*" A short, heavyset man with a mass of gray hair barreled toward us. "*Signor* Brown, *Signora* Brown, *buongiorno*. I was hoping to find you here still." He held out a package to the Browns. "Still warm, it is. It's the bread I told you about yesterday, the one we make only on Wednesdays. Smell. Breathe it in deeply, the artichokes, the pesto, is it not *buono*?" He opened the end of the bag and lifted it to each of our noses. My mouth watered. It did smell *buono.*

"Jock," the man said to Mr. MacLeod, "if I had known you were here with the boy, I would have brought some for you. Malcolm, you come round to my shop this afternoon. I will give you a loaf."

Beside me Malcolm tensed. He looked at the Browns and then at his father.

"Thank you, Nunzio. He will that," Mr. MacLeod said.

"Mr. MacLeod," Aunt Susannah called from the front steps. She cocked her head as if she were asking a question.

"Oh, no," I said, wanting the ground to open and swallow me up. "I-I forgot. She told me to ask you if you wanted some breakfast."

"No worries, lassie." Mr. MacLeod winked. "She'll still feed us." He turned to Malcolm. "Are you hungry, laddie?

Your brother can look to the customers a few minutes more."

Malcolm grinned.

"Thank you, Susannah," called Mr. MacLeod. "Go on, Malcolm. I'm to the shop." He took a long gulp of coffee and then handed the mug to his son.

Malcolm hurried to the house and I started to follow. Behind me Mr. MacLeod banged the tools into his metal toolbox. "The man will think I can no run a proper business now that he sees me with my van broken down two days in a row," he muttered.

I turned. Mr. MacLeod was staring at the Browns' rental car. It was moving slowly down the narrow street. The other baker, Nunzio, was in the back seat.

CHAPTER 8

Wednesday, Continued

"No sweat, no sweet. Right, Elizabeth?" Aunt Susannah said as I entered the kitchen. She smiled and placed a washed skillet in the dish drainer.

Gran nodded at me. "You did a proper good job at breakfast."

"Thanks, Gran," I mumbled. It was nice of her to say so. Though I doubted her guests would agree.

Gran tapped the page in the open binder on the table. "We have only three couples comin' in. Alejandra, the new girl, has already set to work on rooms two and eight. Susannah, if you begin room six immediately, then I think we could spare you and Elizabeth after one o'clock."

What was happening after one o'clock? My breath stuck in my throat. Were we going shopping? For the—ugh!—school uniform?

"Gran," Mags said, poking her head in. "The clothes dryer just quit and though I've tried, I can't get it started again."

Gran frowned. "Machines, they do break down."

Out front, an engine kicked over and roared away. The van? Maybe it had just broken down too. Maybe no one had tampered with it. Maybe. Probably.

The broken dryer threw the whole day off. We had to hang the sheets out to dry in the backyard. Aunt Susannah had to take the towels to the launderette. (Guests, it seems, like sheets crisp, but fuss when their towels crunch.)

Mags and I were put under the command of Thora. If the British have Marines, Thora has been one. She drilled us on how to make beds, vacuum, dust (even the light bulbs) and clean them-until-they-sparkled bathrooms. It was hard work!

The bright spot was that no one mentioned any trips to get my school uniform. I decided not to bring it up either. No sense in putting pressure on anyone.

It was almost 2:30 when Gran found me in the backyard taking down the sheets. "We're needin' more biscuits for the guests' tea this afternoon," she said. "Fetch some. Will you, dear, from the bakery?" She handed me my navy-blue windbreaker and some paper money.

"Sure," I said, putting on the windbreaker.

"The bakery's on Bruntsfield. At the end of our street, go two short blocks up the hill. That busy street will be Bruntsfield. Turn right. Go another block and a half. MacLeod's is not quite to the middle of that block. I think three dozen biscuits will do."

I tapped my fingers nervously against my thigh. Had I got all those directions?

Gran eyed me over her glasses. "Are you feelin' unwell?"

"No. No, Gran. I'm fine. Maybe Mags would like to go too. Where is she?"

"Your sister's to the launderette to help Susannah fetch back the towels."

I turned the money over in my hands. It had the number twenty and a picture of a knight sitting on his horse. I took a shuddering breath. How would I know if I got the right change?

"It's a twenty pound note," Gran said. "Ask Malcolm to wait on you."

"Biscuits, right?"

She smiled and started into the house. Then she stopped. "We don't need them until half three, so if you want to walk about a bit, you may."

"Half what?"

"Three thirty."

"Oh." I bit my lip. "I'll wait until Mags and I can do it together."

"Please yourself."

All the way down Gran's street, I kept hoping Mags would appear. Then she and I could go find the bakery together. But she didn't come. I even stood for a while at the end of the street, watching for her. Finally there was nothing to do but go alone. I told myself I could do it. I told myself again. My stomach churned—it didn't believe me.

After climbing to the top of the hill, I came to the busiest street I had ever seen. Cars, double-decker buses, and taxis whizzed by. The sidewalks were filled with people, hurrying and going in and out of little stores. I tipped my head back. Above the stores the buildings went up four stories. The street had to be Bruntsfield, I decided. A sign on a building said it was. Whew!

I turned and started walking. Fast at first, but then they hit my nose—the most wonderful smells. Cheese from a cheese store. Candles from a candle store. Candy in a chocolate store. Someone came out of a restaurant and I licked my lips as I smelled spicy Indian food. I couldn't wait for my nose to tell me that I had reached the bakery. But I walked and walked.

I began to get nervous. Where was the bakery? Had I missed it? I turned around and retraced my steps, looking more carefully at each store. Most were tiny, some only three giant steps wide, and their fronts were each painted a different color—green, red, yellow, royal blue.

I passed small grocery stores and restaurants and a bicycle store and a bath store and a card store. Across the street was a big park. But no bakery. There wasn't a bakery anywhere! I came to the street I had come up from Gran's. Suddenly, the computer in my brain booted. I had gone left when probably Gran had told me to turn right. Pathetic!!! How was I going to get along here if I couldn't even follow simple directions? I checked my watch—3:00. I still had a half hour. I charged into the next block.

A woman holding a little boy's hand came out of a candy shop. She wore a pink sweatshirt that said San Francisco across the front. I sighed. Why couldn't I be there, not here? Two girls about my age strolled past. They were talking and laughing and eating ice cream. I wished so bad that Krissy were here. If she were, then we would have been talking and laughing and eating ice cream too.

I folded my upper lip into my mouth to keep from crying and crossed into the next block. I turned and walking backward, watched the two girls. All of a sudden, bam—I collided into a pretty, dark-haired woman.

"I'm sorry," I said. She rushed past, hardly noticing. I totally stood still. I knew her, didn't I? But Mags had warned me that when you travel, people can look familiar because you hope they are.

I stared at the woman's back. Her black hair was pulled into a braid that reached almost to her waist. The braid bumped against her back as she sprinted down the street. I grinned. I did know her. Well, sort of. She worked for Gran at the B&B. Her name was Alejandra. Awesome. I had actually seen someone I knew.

CHAPTER 9

Wednesday, 3:10

Three doors down from the corner, I came to a wide store. The framing was painted computer-screen blue and MacLeod's was written in gold lettering across one of the large windows. Yes—the bakery!

A bell tinkled as I pushed open the glass door. The smell hit me immediately—sweet stuff like sugar cookies and spices and chocolate. Yum. I wanted to live there—forever!

Turning, I took it all in. Along the side wall, loaves of different kinds of bread lay in bins and on shelves. An almost empty case of rolls and popovers ran along in front of it. On the back wall were two see-into refrigerators with several yummy-looking cakes in them. A long counter with a cash register on it was in front of the fridges. And underneath, underneath that counter—my mouth watered just looking at the stuff—was a case filled with all kinds of cookies, small tarts, and candies. Too wonderful!

No one was in the store or behind the counter, but there was a fierce argument going on in a back room. Something about wrong orders. Suddenly a teenage boy about Mags' age stormed out from there. He passed me and, after yanking at the entrance door so hard the glass rattled, went out to the street.

"Jamie, wait. It's no what I meant," Mr. MacLeod called and then rushed out after him. On the sidewalk he caught up with Jamie. The street door closed so I couldn't hear their conversation. I didn't know whether I should watch or not. I watched.

Jamie was way angry. He couldn't even get into his jacket. Finally he threw it down and started to walk away. Mr. MacLeod must have been a good persuader because Jamie stopped and nodded. Mr. MacLeod walked toward him.

"Is there somethin' you want?" a voice asked behind me.

I turned. Embarrassed, I pulled at my hair. Malcolm looked at me, his eyes a little hard.

"I-I. Um, Gran sent me to—"

A bell tinkled. "Give me a break, son," said Mr. MacLeod to Jamie as they entered the store. "Let's get through these next few days. When we get the contract, everythin' will be better."

Jamie sighed. "Aye, Da." He still didn't look happy, but he walked with Mr. MacLeod into the back room.

"My grandmother wants three dozen biscuits," I said to Malcolm.

He slid open the door on a cabinet with fancy cookies. "Which would you like?"

"Those are biscuits? I'd like a dictionary that would help me understand the words here."

"We don't sell dictionaries. For that you'll need the bookstore. End of the block." Malcolm jerked his thumb and smiled.

I smiled back. "You choose and tell me what they are," I said.

Malcolm made a cardboard box and began putting cookies from the case in it. He chose flakey cakies, made from chocolate and cornflakes. He put in some brownie-like squares, except they were white. He called them toffee yogurt slices.

The bell tinkled.

Malcolm looked toward the door and smiled. "Rory, be with you in a sec," he said and then turned back to me. "You may also want some lemon tangy slices with chocolate on top and some empire biscuits." He pointed to a sandwich-like "biscuit" with white icing and a cherry in the center.

Rory sniffed loudly like his nose was really stuffed up. "Is Jock in the back?" he asked.

It was an odd question. I had seen Rory standing on the sidewalk, watching the argument between Mr. MacLeod and Jamie.

"Da," Malcolm called, "Rory wants a word."

Mr. MacLeod came out.

"Jock," Rory said, "I thought I would come 'round. See if you need an extra hand."

"You're no workin' for Nunzio anymore?" Mr. MacLeod asked.

"I am, but I could help you in m'off hours. I thought with the Food Fete comin' up..."

"Kind of you to offer, but thank you, no."

Rory cleared his throat. "I could use the money, Jock, if you know what I mean."

"I do, mate. I wish I could help."

"If you change your mind, ring me, will you?"

Mr. MacLeod nodded.

"Cheers." Rory put up a hand and left.

I waited until the door had closed and then took a chance. "What's a food fete?" I asked Malcolm.

He didn't laugh at me. "It's a gatherin' of bakers, jelly makers as well," he explained. "They give out samples to buyers from stores and restaurants. If the buyers like the food, they order it for their establishments. Mr. Brown, who's stayin' at your grandmother's guesthouse, he's a buyer. There's an important fete beginning on Sunday. M'dad will be offering some of our specialties."

"It sounds exciting," I said, handing him the paper money.

Malcolm nodded. He gave me some coins in change and then handed me the two boxes of "biscuits."

I smiled big. I had done it. Maybe I would do all right in Edinburgh.

CHAPTER 10

Wednesday Night

From: Krissy Fong
Subject: Own EM Address
To: Libby Carlsen <libby1@shepherd-house.serve.co.uk>

Hey, GF,

Look!!!! I have my own EM address. Mom said it was "sensible." I think it's completely sensational!!! Besides that nothing, NOTHING is happening here. Life is boring, boring, BOR-ING without u. Yesterday I went swimming at Amanda's. It was OK. I wished it was u, though. I slept over and we watched dvds until her mother told us we were making too much noise and we had to keep it down, down, down because she had to work the next day. :(

AFN BFF,

Krissy :)

It didn't sound all that boring to me. What I had been doing—THAT sounded boring. I went to find Mags. Maybe we could take the telescope up to the park on Bruntsfield. I met her flying down the stairs. She was wearing her suede jacket and the long forest-green scarf that she thought made her look incredible. Which it did.

"What's happening?" I asked.

"Claire's."

(Claire was also seventeen and lived in another B&B down the block. Mags had met her that afternoon and guess what? They had become "buds." We had heard all about it at dinner.)

"Cool," I said, taking the stairs two at a time. "I just need a jacket."

"Wait a minute." Mags yelled after me. She shook her head. "Sorry, not tonight, Libby."

I came back down the stairs. "But at home you let me hang out with you and your friends."

"Yes, at home. And only sometimes. Not now. NOT tonight. But Lib, Claire knows lots of people. I'm sure some of them have younger sisters. I'll ask her. She can bring one of them 'round. Got to go. Cheers."

"Cheers?" I frowned, following her down the stairs with my eyes. CHEERS? What was this "cheers" thing? What was my sister trying to do? Become a Scot? I smacked the banister. Mags was making friends, having a great time and leaving me out. "Thanks, Mags, for coming along and helping me," I muttered, stomping up the stairs.

In my room I cleaned the lens on my telescope. It wasn't dark enough to see any planets or stars. I would have to wait. Suddenly, coming from Gran's parking lot, I heard footsteps and a hushed voice. I looked out the window. Three guys were walking around the van kind of quiet like. I tore down the stairs into the kitchen.

"Aunt Susannah, some guys are sneaking around Mr. MacLeod's van," I said, panting.

"Stay here," she ordered.

She returned in what seemed like an hour. By the clock it was only a few minutes.

"Jamie MacLeod and two of his friends will be sleepin' in the van tonight. It's only a precaution. But thank you for keepin' a lookout."

I nodded, though I felt completely stupid. I headed back to my room. Gran's ginger cat was stretched out across the first stair.

"Sunshine, would you like to see a planet?" I asked, stroking her back. I took her purring as a yes, scooped her up, and together we counted the forty-seven stairs to my room.

In my room I held her up to the telescope and explained how it worked. I told her how amazing the moon looks when you see it through a telescope. She wasn't all that impressed. Squirming from my arms, she jumped to the floor and then up on my bed.

"Thanks a lot, Cat." I said, flopping down beside her. Sunshine stretched out and closed her eyes. "OK, I'll wake you when it's darker. You're right. It will be more exciting then." I scratched her head. In answer she flicked her tail and rolled onto her back. I rubbed her belly.

I glanced at the window. It was amazing how light it still was and how light it would be for a while. I began scanning the room for a book or a magazine, but gave it up in a nanosecond. I felt too fidgety for reading. I got up and pointed the telescope at the apartment building beyond the school.

Someone was standing in a bay window on the fourth floor. I focused the lens. It was a girl and she was using binoculars. She was looking my way. She smiled slowly, smirked really. Then she lifted her hand and waved. Embarrassed, I pulled the drapes.

CHAPTER 11

Thursday

A unt Susannah wiped her hands on a dish towel and fixed her eyes on me. "Today it will have to be, my dear. The dryer is not repaired, but no matter. Thora and Alejandra have agreed to work late. So in the afternoon we will go to town to purchase your school uniform.

I shot Mags my best pleading look.

She shook her head. "They're only clothes," she whispered. (That was from someone who won't wear last year's jeans.) "A lot of kids wear uniforms over here," she continued. "You'll fit in."

I glared at her. Who said I wanted to fit in!

The wind came up in the afternoon—a fierce, demanding, knock-you-down kind of wind. The sky overhead went from gray to black. It spit at us as Aunt Susannah and I boarded the crowded bus. "Perfect," I grumbled, watching the rain dribble down the bus windows. "Absolutely perfect!"

Marks & Spencer on Princes Street in downtown Edinburgh was the store for school uniforms. A salesclerk in her own uniform, a navy print dress, directed us to gray wool skirts, gray wool sweaters, and white blouses. Boring!

I took a set of what we decided could be my size into a dressing room and changed. Stepping out from the curtain, I stared at myself in the mirror on the wall. Ugh!

"Grim. Gray is a decidedly grim color," said a voice behind me.

I turned. A girl with short hair cocked her head and studied my outfit.

"But on you, it is not half bad." She flicked me a smile. Then she shifted her gaze beyond me to the mirror and pulled her stylishly cut hair toward her cheeks. "Gray is exceedingly not my color."

I studied the girl. Cute, she was about my age, but a head shorter. She had blue eyes and great skin. She was the girl from last night, the one with the binoculars.

"I finally convinced my mum to let me off this year. Of course, next year, I'll have to wear one—a uniform. All the best schools do. You goin' to Bruntsfield Primary this term?"

I nodded.

"Me, too. Is it your telescope or does it belong to someone else?"

"It's mine."

"Excellent. By the by, I'm Philippa Armstrong. Phil. Everybody calls me Phil. Except my mum, who insists on calling me Pippa, which I abhor. It's hideous. I'm not in nursery."

"I'm—"

"You're Elizabeth Carlsen and you're from the States." She smiled smugly. "I just love America."

"Oh, you've been there?"

"No, but I'm goin'. I'm goin' to be an actress, a film star. I'm goin' to live in California. Malibu, I expect." She side-stepped to get a better look at herself in the mirror. She frowned and pointed to the navy-blue parka vest she had on. "What do you think? Not smashing, I know. I was keen for lime green or hot pink, but Mum said it was Marks & Spencer or nothing. Good value for your money."

I noticed the tag hanging from the zipper. It said, "shower resistant." I was sure they weren't worn in the shower. "Change out of that," Phil ordered. "I've got a brilliant idea."

I shrugged and walked back toward the curtain. I glanced over my shoulder. Like a dart, Phil was headed for Aunt Susannah, who was choosing socks.

When I came out of the dressing room, Aunt Susannah looked a little bewildered. People often looked that way around Phil I soon learned.

"Pippa," Aunt Susannah said, (For a whole thirty seconds I didn't know who she was talking about. Then I got it—Phil. Aunt Susannah meant Phil.) "says that almost no one in level seven wears uniforms. Your grandmother and I would no want you to feel out of place. So I think you should wear your clothes from home. No reason to spend money unnecessarily. If you want a uniform later, we'll be able to purchase one, I'm sure."

"Absolutely," I said, trying to keep my face serious.

Phil stood out of Aunt Susannah's view. Her smile was as wide as a banner. Then she slipped beside me. "Would it be all right, Miss Stewart, if Elizabeth helped me finish my shopping? We can get home on the bus. I do it all the time."

"That sounds lovely. What do you say, Elizabeth?" Aunt Susannah asked.

"Sure. If it's OK with you."

Aunt Susannah opened her purse and then handed me some coins. "Four. We'll be expectin' you around four o'clock."

I put the money in my jeans' pocket and nodded.

"Excellent," Phil said, grabbing my arm and leading me away.

"Cheers," I said to Aunt Susannah.

CHAPTER 12

Thursday, Continued :) !!!!

Phil led me to a counter across the room. The sign above it read Pay Point. I got it—understood what it meant. It was the checkout counter. I nearly did a dance right there.

Phil paid for the parka as if she'd been doing this kind of thing forever. I was awed. At home my friends and I never even went into a department store without a mom.

"That finishes my shopping," Phil said and reached for my arm. "Let's get out of here, Elizabeth."

"Call me Libby," I said. "Everyone in California calls me Libby."

Phil flashed a smile. "Absolutely, Libby. I'm famished. You must be too and I know the perfect place."

She pulled me down one flight of stairs and rushed me down another. Then she dragged me through the men's department, up the escalator, through another department and out onto a brick-paved street. Being with Phil was like riding a roller coaster. I felt scared and excited at the same time.

The brick-paved street was really an alley, but with no cars. There was a crush of people, however—tourists with cameras and Scottish mothers pushing baby strollers. They were all going in and out of the big department stores, cafes, and small stores.

Phil ran me through the crowds like a pro. She played soccer, and on a winning team, I was sure of it. Finally she turned a corner and stopped in front of an ochre-colored building.

"Ta-da," she said, spreading her arms out dramatically. She pointed to the sign above her head.

BURGER KING Restaurant. It was Burger King!

"I thought you might be a little homesick," Phil said.

She was right. I walked in the doors and sighed a big sigh. The place smelled like California sunshine.

We ordered. Phil helped me with the money.

"This way," she said after our trays were full. She led me up a long, circular staircase and to a large room that was nearly all glass on two sides. I nearly dropped my tray. Above the treetops, high on the hill was a castle just like in a storybook.

"Wow! Does anyone live there?"

"Some soldiers, but mostly it's a museum. Impressive, though. The queen stays at the other end of the Royal Mile. At her palace, Holyrood. She holds a garden party there every June. Very posh. I intend to be invited someday."

At the far end of the room someone laughed. I knew that laugh. I turned. Mags was seated among seven or so other teenage boys and girls. I started toward an empty table near them.

Suddenly Mags looked at me. She shook her head slightly and scowled. I froze. She didn't want me to sit with her? My own sister didn't want me to sit with her? To spite her I wanted to plop myself down at that table anyway.

Phil clucked at my shoulder. "They think they own the world, don't they? Never mind, let's sit over here." Using her tray Phil pointed to a table at the window facing the castle.

I shot Mags an angry look, which she didn't even see—she was so busy talking to her new friends—and followed Phil.

"The redhead is your sister, right?" Phil swirled her straw in her drink.

I nodded.

"She's pretty. And she's landed in the best crew. Charisma. I would say, she has charisma. I don't have a sister. Nor a brother. No father either. What's it like to have a sister?"

"It's the pits."

Phil set the French fries between us and dipped one in some catsup. I dipped another. We ate for several minutes in silence.

"The trouble with being their age is that you can think you are the world," Phil said. "Claire, with the blond braid—" Phil used a French fry to indicate the girl sitting next to Mags. "She's pretty, clever with school stuff and has a smart way about clothes. Drives the lads mad when she plays the harp, looks like a mermaid with her hair flowin' down. But she's oblivious to anythin' else—I mean life. She couldn't see it if she were bifocaled. She—" Phil broke off.

A boy, an older boy, about seventeen, sauntered across the room to the group. I had seen him before. Phil glued her eyes to him. Her lips parted and stayed that way.

"Tady," she said with a sigh. "Jamie MacLeod is definitely tady."

"What?"

"Tady, you know, like sweepin' up."

I had to think for a minute. "Oh, tidy?"

"Yes, easy on the eyes."

I agreed. Some movie producer would think Jamie MacLeod was blue star quality. Muscular arms, tallish, sandy hair, graceful—the guy definitely had teen idol potential. Casually he pulled up a chair, straddled it, and zeroed in on my sister.

"Fancies her, I would say," Phil said.

It figured. I bit into my cheeseburger and chewed.

Suddenly Phil leaned forward, her eyes bright. "There's somethin' goin' on at the MacLeod's bakery. Trouble of some kind."

I stopped eating and sat back in my chair. Should I tell her about the van—the boys sleeping in it last night?

She took a quick bite of her burger. "What time do you have?" she asked her mouth still full. Then not waiting for my answer, she glanced at her own watch. "Wrap up that sandwich," she ordered. She sucked noisily on the straw in her drink, wrapped her half-eaten burger and grabbed her package. She bolted for the stairs.

When I didn't follow, she turned and gestured excitedly. I looked at Mags wistfully and downed my cola. Still munching my burger, I took the stairs two at a time.

Phil ran me the length of what I later learned was Princes Street and then across North Bridge. Below the bridge a train rumbled at the bottom of a deep ravine.

"Phil, where are we going?" I yelled as I dodged a group of people who were wearing costumes and handing out flyers.

"I'll tell you in a moment when there's time. We don't want to be late."

"Late for what and how far are we going?" I panted, trying to stay up with her as we climbed a hill. She didn't answer but pulled me across a cobblestone street. A bus, a double-decker one, roared past us.

"Couldn't we take one of those?"

"It's not much farther. You don't walk much, do you?" she said, taking the lead and threading us through the heavy crowds.

It started to drizzle. Around me black umbrellas popped open and I was caught in a sea of turtles. Phil didn't seem to mind the rain or the umbrellas. She plowed us down the narrow sidewalk of the long street, crossed to the next and stopped on the corner.

I shivered, shaking icy drops from my hair. "Is this where we catch the bus?" I asked hopefully.

"No," she said and smiled mysteriously. "This is where we catch—"

The sky cracked open and it poured.

"Come on," Phil said, propelling me into a store. "We'll keep an eye out from in here."

The store was a bookstore. One of my favorite places. It must have been one of Phil's too.

"Hello, Pippa," a salesgirl said. "Chuckin' down, isn't it?"

Phil (evidently still known as Pippa by a lot more people than her mother) flashed a smile, nodded, and led the way into a corner room. It had big picture windows. We had a perfect view of the street.

"What are we watching for?" I asked.

"Malcolm, Malcolm MacLeod. He takes piping lessons in the flat across the way. He finishes just about now."

"How do you know?"

Phil smiled, rather smugly I thought. "My mum has the copy shop next to the bakery. I run errands for her. And of course, I watch and listen to people. Have you noticed that adults talk sometimes as if you were no in view, even though you're right there?" She shook her head. "It does worry me that. An actress must have stage presence. My dramatic teacher says so. If people behave as if you are invisible, how much presence can a person truly have?"

I didn't have an answer. But I found it very hard to believe that anyone could find Philippa Armstrong invisible.

"Why are we waiting for Malcolm?" I asked.

"We want to talk with him. Question him."

"About what?"

"The goings-on at his father's bakery."

"Oh." I chewed a nail. The idea of questioning Malcolm about his father's business made my insides squirmy. I inched away from Phil. Could I find my way to Gran's from here by myself? I scanned the room. Where could I get a map or something?

The shelves to my left were filled with science books. No map there, but a large navy-blue book was titled *Stargazers, The Story of the Telescope*. Eagerly I took it down and began flipping through.

I stopped at a picture of a Herschel telescope. It was incredible. Encased in wood, built around 1760. The telescope had been used by amateur astronomers, the caption said. The caption also said the one in the picture was in the Royal Museum of Scotland, Edinburgh. A Herschel telescope was here!! In Edinburgh!! "Phil, where is the Royal—?"

"Hello, Pippa," said another salesgirl. "We've the new mystery by Catherine Finch downstairs. And," she said with a wink, "*Great Ladies of the Screen* was just unboxed."

"There he is," Phil whispered to me. "Thank you, Susan, but it will need to be another time." Phil grabbed my arm, her eyes big with excitement. "We're off," she crowed and pulled me out the door.

CHAPTER 13

Thursday Afternoon, Continued :(

Jumping over puddles, the rain still hitting us in the face, we tore across the intersection. Ahead of us, Malcolm marched up the street, swinging a large wooden case. We didn't catch up with him until halfway up the block. He glanced at us and frowned slightly.

"I'm showin' Edinburgh to Libby," Phil said. "This is Libby. Have you met her?"

I tugged at the ends of my hair. The rain, which was now only a drizzle, had plastered it to down. I was sure I now looked like a pinhead.

Malcolm smiled at me, a quiet, friendly smile. I smiled back. "Aye, I've met her. And, Pippa, you probably know I've met her. You've probably been watchin' us through those binoculars of yours."

Phil didn't even blush. She just plunged in. "Your father's from Skye, is he not?" she asked, keeping step with Malcolm.

"Aye."

"His brother still lives there, does he not?"

"And why would you want to know?"

"I heard he had a brother."

Malcolm snorted and swung his case faster. "You heard wrong. He has no brother. Only two sisters. Does that satisfy you?"

"Then it must be a cousin."

"A cousin what?" Malcolm stopped walking and put his case down. He pushed his hair back from his eyes and, squaring his shoulders, dared her to continue. Which she did.

"A cousin, I think, who is tryin' to sabotage the bakery."

"I think you're away with the fairies. That's what I think."

I stared at the ground. Phil was really embarrassing. Did Malcolm believe I was like her just because I was with her? I looked away.

Across the street was a three-story stone building with statutes on its roof. At least a dozen steps climbed to the building's important looking entrance. I read the gold lettering over the door—Royal Museum of Scotland.

"Hey, that's the museum where they have inventions," I blurted out.

Malcolm turned to me. "Yes, they have many. Are you interested—?"

Phil interrupted. "Someone is tryin' to hurt your father's business. The things that have been happenin', they're part of a plot."

Malcolm scowled, picked up his case and strode up the street.

Phil was not going to be left in the dust. Grabbing my arm, she ran after him.

"It's usually a male—a brother or cousin," she persisted. "Sure it's some kind of feud between them. It's a distant cousin maybe. Someone your father wronged a long time ago and now he's takin' his revenge. It all makes sense."

"You're crazy is what makes sense. M'dad's no carrin' on a feud with anyone. And there's no plot. Just a Miss Nosey Parker with a love for stirrin' things up." He whirled on his heel and stomped away.

A white and red double-decker bus pulled up to the bus stop in front of us. In the section above the driver's window was a large 23. I read the names next to the 23, hoping one of them would be Bruntsfield. None of them were.

"Here's the bus," Phil called to Malcolm. "Aren't you gettin' on?"

Malcolm kept walking, his shoulders squared, his head high. Phil frowned. Then she steered me toward the line of waiting people. "There's a plot, you can be sure of that," she whispered. "He just doesn't want to admit it."

I nodded, but I wasn't really listening. I was worrying about the bus. I stared at the coins I had taken from my pocket. Did I have enough? Which ones was I supposed to put in?

Phil pulled a red plastic wallet-type thing from her purse and flipped it open. She showed it to the bus driver. He nodded. Then jerking her thumb at me, Phil said,

"American. I'm payin' her fare." She dropped coins in the box and smiled back at me. I sighed with gratitude.

From a red box across the aisle she pulled down a white ticket and handed it to me. "If you don't have one when the inspector gets on to check, he'll fine you and throw you off the bus."

I shuddered and tightened my grip on the ticket.

"Does the inspector do that in the States?" she asked, as we climbed the corkscrew staircase.

"I don't know," I said.

She slid into an empty double seat. (It was red plaid, BTW.) "You don't ride the buses much in the States?" she asked.

"Not much." I wasn't going to tell her that before today the only bus I had ever ridden was a school bus. And that was only on field trips.

❧   ❧

"Scoot out," Phil said, nudging me out of the seat and then sliding past me. "We're comin' up on our stop." Did she mean home? In a flash of terror, it occurred to me she might not. I raced after her to ask, but the bus stopped and she was out the door. The only thing for me to do was get off too.

As the engine revved and the bus sped away, I panicked. Where was I? Behind me was an apartment building. Across the street was a flower store and next to it a vegetable-and-fruit store. I studied them. Had I seen them before? They looked familiar. The store next to them was a corner grocery store. We were on Bruntsfield. Yes! We were only a few blocks from Gran's. Yes! I knew my way back to the B&B. Oh, yes! Yes! Yes! Who would think that a flower shop and a fruit-and-vegetable store could look so good?

A woman with a long black braid hurried past those stores and turned the corner—Alejandra. She was carrying some boxes. I recognized the boxes. They were from MacLeod's. Yum. Gran must have needed more "biscuits."

"Come on," Phil yelled, standing halfway down the block. She dashed across the street. I ran and arrived at the crosswalk just as the beeping of the traffic light started. I looked to my left. The way was clear. I stepped off the sidewalk into the street. From behind me somebody took hold of my jacket and jerked me back to the curb. A taxi cab whizzed past, missing my toes by inches. My legs became spaghetti and my breath came in little gasps.

"Dear, you got to mind the traffic," said the woman who had grabbed me.

I nodded and shuddered. The light changed again. I just stood there—frozen. People walked around me and started across. Phil ran over. "Yank, that was dead scary," she said, taking my arm and hustling me into the street. "Here, you have to look right and then left. This is Scotland, not America."

I swallowed hard and swung my head like a windshield wiper.

"You'll get on though, I'm sure," Phil said reassuringly.

We arrived safely at the sidewalk.

"Come meet my mum."

"No," I jerked my head. "I-I need to get back to Gran's. To help set up the tea stuff." I wasn't sure if Gran needed me or not. I just knew I needed to go back to the B&B. And NOW.

Phil looked disappointed, but then brightened. "Why not come over after dinner? I'll come 'round and get you."

I nodded. What was wrong with me?! Why did I do that?!

CHAPTER 14

Thursday, Tea Time

I was mad at myself all the way back to Gran's. Why had I said I would go to Phil's? Why hadn't I said, "No"? Or even, "I'll have to ask"? Why??!! Sure, Phil was fun. And interesting. And someone to be with. But she was scary too. I felt like I was jumping off the high dive when I was with her. And hoping there was water below.

Flopping down on Gran's front stairs, I dropped my chin into my hands. How could I get out of going to Phil's after dinner? Maybe I could get Gran to say no for me. Or maybe Mags and I could decide to do something together—go to the movies? Not! Sunshine trotted across the parking lot and brushed up against my leg. I scratched her between the ears. She purred and rolled on to her side. I scratched her belly and she stretched out her paws, flexed and purred even louder. This could mean trouble. Should I keep scratching?

The day before, Sunshine had left a large dead bird on the steps. A wee giftee for Gran. Cats, Gran had told me, did that bit of kindness for their friends. They knew humans were terrible hunters. Sunshine and I were getting to be friends. Was she soon going to leave a dead bird on my bed? I tapped my fingers against my thigh. Friendships could be tricky.

The gate clanged and I looked up. It was Alejandra. Her mouth twitched into a fast smile. Then she hurried inside. I followed her with my eyes. She was carrying the boxes from the bakery.

I licked my lips, thinking about what was in those boxes. Whatever problems I was having in Scotland, I was having no problem with their cookies. I gave Sunshine's fur a smoothing and went in search of goodies. What a lovely custom tea was!

"Dear, you're not to worry," Gran was saying into the phone as I pushed open the door to the kitchen. "They're fine."

"We're only workin' them twenty hours a day." Aunt Susannah yelled toward the phone and then winked at me.

I stopped in my tracks, my heart pounding.

"You want to speak to your mum?" Gran asked.

I tried not to grab the phone. Sudden tears made the room blurry.

"Libby, how are you doin'?" Mom asked.

I sniffled. "Fine, Mom, I'm fine."

"Gran told me you saw a bit of the city today. Lovely, isn't it?"

I went into a sulk. "It's OK," I murmured. I know. I know. I could have said that I saw the castle and that it was awesome. But I wasn't going to let my mom think that they had made the right decision sending me here. Because they hadn't.

If a person could hear frowning, I heard it when my mom said, "Libby, I know it's goin' to be an adjustment for you. But you might try to see it all as an adventure."

I sighed.

"Lillibet, really, you're goin' to do fine. Susannah said you made a friend."

"Well, maybe."

"Daddy and I are praying for you, Libby," Mom said softly.

I didn't know what to say to that. Well, I knew what I wanted to say, but I didn't think my mom would hear it and not give me a lecture.

"I'm leavin' in an hour for my training retreat. Daddy is already there. We'll call you again when we get back. Oh, I almost forgot. Tom said, 'Thanks for making his bed.' I didn't know you did that. It was nice of you, dear. He also told me to tell you that your newsy e-mails are wonderful and you should keep sending them."

"OK," I said. What *newsy e-mails was he talking about?!* Oh, got it. He was being sarcastic.

"I've only one room left to pack. Are you quite certain you don't want a stuffed toy or two? I could send them with your clothes," my mom said.

I bit my lip. "I'm certain." But I wasn't. I imagined my room, my house, with only its furniture. A big rock formed in my throat. I felt so lost, empty. "Mom, I love you."

"We love you too. Tell Mags I'm sorry I missed her."

I gave the phone to Aunt Susannah and trudged out into the hall. I was halfway up to the landing when I remembered Thora. While I had been talking to my mom, I had watched Thora filling plates with cookies. She had marched out of the kitchen and would have carried them into the breakfast room for the guests' tea time. I turned and bounded down the steps. Just because I was miserable didn't mean I shouldn't eat.

The German guy, the one who had insisted on whole wheat toast, was coming out of the breakfast room. He had two flakey cakies in one hand and a toffee yogurt slice in the other. So much for being a health food nut!

The American couple, the Browns, were sitting at a table, drinking tea and poring over sightseeing brochures. Between them they had a plate of goodies. From the serving table I took a napkin and scooped up two empire biscuits.

"Join us," Mrs. Brown said and pointed to the empty chair across from her. Smiling at me, she reached for the half-eaten empire biscuit on her plate, brought it to her mouth, blinked and then put it down. She picked up a lemon bar and bit into it. "Um-mm, delicious," she said.

I decided I would go back for a lemon bar.

I bit into an empire biscuit. Ugh, it wasn't sweet. It was salty. Very salty. I looked it over. The empire biscuit I had eaten yesterday hadn't tasted like that. I folded it into my napkin and bit into the other one. Yuck! What was the matter with them?

CHAPTER 15

Thursday Evening, So Much Happening!!!

Gran called the bakery immediately. I overheard part of the conversation—the part where she was majorly upset. But then she noticed me listening and sent me out of the kitchen. I wish grown-ups wouldn't do that.

After dinner I was e-mailing my brother, telling him again that nothing was happening except that I had met Phil, when Phil showed up. She was wearing pink-and-purple sequined shoes and an I-told-you-so smile.

She dragged me into the breakfast room. "The whole of Bruntsfield is buzzin' about the bakery's troubles."

I wondered if everybody was talking or if Phil was talking to everybody.

She clucked her tongue. "Mr. MacLeod, though, he still says there's no difficulty, just someone's mistakes.

"It could be a mistake," I protested. "It's easy to mistake salt for sugar. We did it in our scout project once."

Phil's mouth twisted. "Not to a baker. My mother's a painter. One time she asked me to put a dab of ultramarine blue on her pallet. I was not paying attention and squeezed a dab from the cobalt blue tube. She knew straight away. Bakin' is no doubt the same. Then take into account a van that never breaks down, breakin' down two days in a row. A wrong order that is placed with the egg and butter man. No order is placed for flour. What does it all add up to?"

"The flour order was Jamie MacLeod's fault," I said. Phil's face was a question mark. "I was in the bakery yesterday afternoon," I explained. "I overheard an argument."

Phil blinked, then grinned slowly. "What else do you know?"

"Just that," I said. But a thought nudged me.

"OK," Phil said, "but what of the other mishaps? Were they all just coincidences, a bit of bad luck?"

"There's no such thing as luck. God's in control of ..." My voice trailed off. "My mother says—" I stopped and pulled my bottom lip over my upper. I couldn't believe I had said that. It sounded so "churchie." I pretended to clean a smudge on the table, bracing myself. Phil, I was sure, was going to make fun of me the way some of my school friends did when I said stuff like that. I waited. Nothing happened. Phil had cocked her head like people do when they're examining something. Then she shrugged.

"Nice room this," she said, looking around.

I looked around too. She was right. White walls, mahogany fireplace, mahogany tables, pictures of flowers and fields and people on horseback, a forest-green rug. It felt clean and woodsy and peaceful.

Phil smiled crookedly. "And to think this is the scene of the latest crime." She dropped to her hands and knees. Suddenly she reached toward something under the table behind me. She stood up. Between her thumb and middle finger she held a crumb. "Appears to be part of a biscuit, wouldn't you say?" Her eyes glistened. Her face was flushed. "Where are they now—the empire biscuits? We should examine them."

"Gran took them back to the bakery."

"Oh." She sighed. Phil ran her eyes around the room again. "I've been havin' a think on this. They've no new employees. I asked. So perhaps it's not, as they say in American films, 'an inside job.'" Phil made air quotes. "But maybe someone's sneakin' in nights and troublin' things." Her eyes danced. "I've a brilliant thought. Will your grandmother let you come for a sleepover at my flat tonight?"

"I guess."

"Good. Bring your telescope. We'll set it up in my bedroom and keep watch from there. My window faces the dryin' greens. And at the edge of those greens are the shops on Bruntsfield and the bakery."

I wasn't convinced Phil was putting the pieces of it together in the right way. But I was intrigued.

As we walked upstairs to pick up my telescope and stuff, after Gran said I could sleep over, which was after she called Phil's mom and checked that it was OK. (My mom does that. I guess the rules here are the same. But I was surprised that Gran even knew Phil's mom.) Anyway, climbing the stairs I flashed on being in the bakery yesterday. I had noticed something odd. I remembered thinking at the time, *That's odd*, but as I walked up the stairs with Phil, I couldn't remember what was odd. Doesn't it just make you crazy when that happens?

CHAPTER 16

More Thursday Evening !!!

Phil's flat was on the fourth floor of a five-floor building. The building didn't have an elevator. It had a lot of stairs that zig and then zag. I tell you about the stairs because I hauled my telescope up them.

"We're here, Mum," Phil called, already on the landing and entering her apartment. She gestured for me to speed it up and then vanished inside.

I found her standing in the doorway of a sun-filled room. The Armstrongs' living room was not what I expected. No carved wood furniture or overstuffed chairs. No lace curtains. No pictures of flowers in vases or a dog looking at a dog as in Gran's living room.

Instead there were paintings with lots of color and shapes that I couldn't figure out hanging on white walls. Stacks of books stood in piles on the mantelpiece and on the floor. A paint-smeared blanket dangled off the arm of a blue plaid couch. In the far corner on a small table was a computer in the off mode.

"Mum." Phil spoke to a dark-haired woman hunched over a table in front of the bay window. "This is Elizabeth Carlsen, Mrs. Stewart's granddaughter.

Phil's mother continued the stroke she was making with her brush. Finished, she cocked her head, studied it and then nodded. She turned to me and smiled. She and Phil had the same wide smile. "Hello, nice to have you visit. Pippa, there's cocoa if you've a mind to make it and some biscuits I bought today."

"Thanks, Mum." Phil grinned and led me down the hall. "I hope they're not empire biscuits," she whispered, her eyes squinching up. She opened a door to the left. "We're still interior decorating. Until a few weeks ago I slept in the box."

I must have looked puzzled.

She pointed to a door back up the hall. "It's a room with no windows, so it's called 'the box.'" Phil made air quotes and grinned. "Beastly small too. Spacious for a mouse. I was gettin' quite claustrophobic. Mum agreed to swap rooms. So I now have this gloriously big thing and I'm dreamin' what to do with it."

The room had a double bed and an armoire and a chest of drawers with a TV on top of it. Phil and her mom were obviously still painting. One wall was partly yellow and mostly dull red. The wall next to it had a large pale blue section. Three strips of different kinds of wallpaper were pinned to another wall. Across from the door was a large window. Phil dragged the table and chair from in front of it off to one side.

"It's perfect, isn't it?" She gestured to the spot she had just vacated. "Set your telescope up there."

I went over to the window and looked out.

"See," Phil said, "those windows near the ground across the dryin' greens. It's good it's evening. During the day women still hang their laundry to dry. Now count over three. The third and fourth windows are the bakery. If you count over five, it's the back of Mum's shop."

"This is great. We'll be able to spot someone going through the back door," I said.

"No back door. The shops have no entrance to the greens."

"We'll spot them climbing through the windows?"

Phil frowned. "That's a bit of a problem as well. Set up the telescope. I'll make the cocoa and see what kind of biscuits Mum bought. Oh, and I've got some sweeties. Wait 'til you try them." She left.

I turned back to the building across the drying greens. The windows on the top floors shone like gold in the setting sun. I let my eyes fall to the shadows below. What kind of problem could there be with the shop windows?

It took only minutes to assemble my telescope. Then I aimed the tube at a bakery window and focused. I couldn't believe it! There were vertical bars on that window. And the other one too! Nobody could crawl through one of them. I had lugged my telescope over here for nothing. This whole thing was a waste of time. No one was getting in the shop. Phil was crazy.

"I squirted a bit of cream on top," Phil said. She handed me a mug and set hers down. "Be back in a tick."

I sipped the chocolate, some of the sweet cream catching on my lip. I sighed and shrugged. We were playing at detective, just playing. But so what? It was something to do.

Phil returned with a plate of cookies and a small wax paper bag. She tore open the bag. "Have a fried egg? They're the rage."

About the size of a large cookie, the candy did look like a fried egg. I took one and bit into it. It tasted faintly lemony. But it chewed like a six-week old marshmallow. If this was what girls ate here, I was going to have problems at sleepover parties.

Phil walked past me to the telescope. "How does this work?"

"Sight along the tube until you find the object you want, like this. Then look in the eyepiece and move the tube until you see the object. Then turn this knob counterclockwise until the object comes into focus."

"Excellent! With this we'll not miss the villain."

"I suppose," I said and frowned.

"What?"

"Phil," I tried to be patient, "how's a villain going to get into the store?"

"I've had a think on that. A key, somebody has a key."

I doubted it. I also doubted that anyone would come tonight like we'd sent them an invitation.

"We could watch the *telly* whilst we wait," she said and frowned. "Or not."

I wanted to say, "Let's watch," but it seemed like Phil didn't want to, so I said, "Let's not."

Phil gave me her widest smile. "Excellent."

Quickly dropping books and papers into piles on the floor, she cleared off the table. She pulled it and the chair over to the bed. "You may sit on the bed or in the chair. I think the bed could be more comfortable," she said, disappearing into the hallway. She returned a few minutes later with a large game box. "How do you feel about--?" Her eyes sparkled.

I stared at the title on the box--Cluedo. I had never heard of it. "Sure," I said, not wanting to disappoint her.

But then Phil took off the lid and opened up the game board. I smiled big. Cluedo was Clue! Wow! I had played it at home a zillion times. This would be fun.

Phil loved the game. She didn't just move her "man." She acted out the characters and invented wild stories about why Mrs. White (or Miss Scarlet or Professor Plum) did it with the lead pipe (or the rope or the knife) in the conservatory (in the hall, in the kitchen). I started making up stories too. I wasn't as good as Phil, but it didn't matter. We got to laughing until my stomach hurt.

Suddenly Phil rocked back in her chair, nearly sending the telescope sprawling. She grabbed it just in time. "Sorry," she said. "Got a bit excited."

"I've forgotten to watch the shop," I confessed.

"I've been glancin' over every now and then. I've noticed nothing suspicious. But I don't expect anything to be happenin' there for a time. Too many people on the street."

I nodded and walked to the window. I searched the darkening sky for stars.

"No stars," I said, not finding any. "Too many clouds."

"What drew you to astronomy?" Phil asked. "I mean, is it something a lot of American kids do? I've not heard that."

"My brother started doing it in 4-H. That's a club. He even built his own telescope. It was so cool. And then there was the part about staying up late and going places—like the mountains and the beach. I got to go if the whole family went. Then two years ago my parents took us to the observatory to see a show. It was awesome. It was about the Christmas Star. After that I had to have my own telescope."

"Cool. Did he—the lecturer—say there was a star?"

"He gave a few possible explanations. A super nova. A cluster of stars, some planets in unusual orbits. But it seemed to me God had planned it, whatever it was, and He made it happen. An astronomer on TV said the stars aren't just randomly there. They have a pattern—a design."

Phil scratched the tip of her nose and then stretched her arms over her head. "Stars may be planned, but nothin' else is. If there is a God—and I don't think there is—He's on holiday, probably the south of France. All the best people go there." She grinned.

I knew I was supposed to say, "No. God is not on holiday. He's watching over us." The problem was I didn't feel like He was—watching over me.

"We need some music," Phil said. She pointed to a stack of CDs in a stand beside her night table. "You choose."

I walked over and smiled. Most of them were musicals. I chose *Cats* and handed it to her.

She purred, "My favorite," and put it in the player. "I'll tell you what. I just bought this new nail varnish. I'll do your nails and then you do mine." She wriggled a hand with a different color on each nail.

I nodded, but squirmed. Was I really up for rainbow nails?

We did Phil's nails first—all of them in apple green. When it was my turn, I just went with it. Apple green did look way cool on Phil's. Phil, who was planning to take voice lessons sometime in the near future, sang along with her CD the whole time. She was good. I joined in, but that's all I'm going to say about my singing. It was fun though. Phil made it fun.

She had some teen fashion magazines and we dove into them. We were in the middle of a quiz about your ideal fashion statement when the yawns started getting me. I stifled one, only to have another start. What time was it? The dog's paws pointed to the "11" and the "6." I lay back on Phil's bed and closed my eyes.

"I'm only closing my eyes for a few minutes," I said to someone shaking my shoulders.

"A few minutes?" The someone shaking me was Phil. "You've been asleep for hours." She was leaning over me. Her eyes were shiny with excitement.

"What is it?" I asked.

She practically leapt over me and raced back to the telescope. Peering into the eyepiece she said, "There's a light movin' about in the shop. See for yourself."

At first I saw nothing. Then I saw it. A small light was moving about like it was searching for something. Abruptly it stopped. "Phil, what do think is happening?"

She was pulling on her jacket. "Someone is there who doesn't want anyone to know." She tossed me my parka. "Come on, he can only get out the front door. We'll surprise him."

CHAPTER 17

Friday, 1:30 in the Morning!!!

Phil was out the hallway and charging down the stairs before I said, "We're not going to try to grab this person, are we?"

"Hurry!" she stage whispered from the landing below and kept going.

I took the stairs as fast as I could. Running after her, I raced out the street door, around the corner and down the long block. For a short person, Phil ran fast. I didn't catch up with her until the telephone booth just before Bruntsfield.

"Listen," I said, trying to catch my breath as we squatted beside the booth, "I'm not going to try to grab this person. It could be dangerous."

"I agree. We'll only see who it is. We'll get a description. No worries."

Good idea! I tingled with excitement.

We made a dash for the corner cafe and flattened ourselves against the building.

"Nothing to this," Phil whispered. She raised an eyebrow. "Can you not imagine what this villain would say if he knew that we—"

"Phil—" I put a finger to my lips. I swallowed hard and pressed my back against the building.

Phil inched farther along the wall. She stopped. We waited, almost not daring to breathe, for the sounds of the saboteur—the tinkling bell of a door and footsteps on the sidewalk.

But I heard nothing. The street was silent except for a few cars going by and some voices a long way off. Phil cleared her throat and jerked her head toward Bruntsfield. We crept to the corner of the building, and hesitating not more than a nanosecond, we peeked around it. I jumped back! Flames! Flames—only a few yards from us—were shooting skyward from big, black bags.

"Fire!" Phil screamed. "Someone set the garbage on fire."

The big plastic bags—I counted three—at the curbside were on fire. Paper napkins and paper cups turned brown, curled, and disintegrated in the flames. The fire leaped to the top of the next bag. Holes opened in the first bag, and a smell, chemically and stinky, hit my nose. The plastic was melting. The bag was breaking apart. Scraps of burning paper escaped from the bags and fluttered upward. The fire was spreading.

"Water, we need water," Phil gasped. She ran to a doorway on the other side of the cafe and began pushing buzzers.

"Fire," she shouted into the intercom. Above us windows banged opened. People stuck their heads out. Some started yelling. Others shot out of the doorway just as the burning cinders caught at the awning above the dress shop next to the bakery.

People carried bowls and threw water at the garbage bags. It helped some. The awning, however, was impossible. It was totally ablaze and flames licked at the wooden facings of the store. In the distance I heard the whoop of sirens coming closer. Blue lights flashing, a red and silver fire truck arrived. A police car swung into the side street and parked next to the phone booth. The crowd moved back to let the firemen work, but nobody left.

The firemen put the fire out quickly. The awning hung in tatters and the front of the dress store was blackened. "Might have been worse," people around me murmured. They coughed and wrinkled their noses at the smell of smoke, burnt cloth and chemicals. "If we'd not been alerted, it might have been much worse."

Mr. MacLeod hurried past me and entered his bakery. Phil nudged me. "Come on, let's tell him—"

Just then two men in navy-blue uniforms with silver buttons approached us. One of them, identified himself as PC Barrows. (PC stands for police constable.)

"I understand," he said to Phil, "you reported the fire."

"Yes."

"And," said the officer turning to me, "you were accompanying her."

"Yes," I said, smiling proudly.

"Please give me your names and your addresses."

We did. He wrote them in a notebook.

"And I found this near the bags," Phil said. She pulled a lighter, the kind you see in a drugstore near the checkout stand, from the pocket of her jacket. She held it with two fingers. "I tried not to smudge the fingerprints, but I may have," she explained.

PC Barrows pursed his lips and removed a handkerchief from his pocket. Triumphantly Phil dropped it there. A look passed between PC Barrows and the other officer.

Phil gasped. "It's not mine. I found it, I say. Over there." She pointed beyond the burned bags. "Someone obviously dropped it."

PC Barrows wrapped the lighter and put it in his pocket. "Yes, thank you. Please remain here with PC Grantham," he said, moving away from us and the crowd. With his free hand he pulled a radio from his belt. He read into the radio from his notebook. After a few moments he nodded, placed the radio back in his belt, and returned.

"We will take you home now," he said.

"That's OK, Officer," I said, trying to be helpful. "Phil only lives around the block. We can walk."

"We will take the two of you home. Please accompany PC Grantham to the car and wait there."

"They think we did it," Phil said under her breath.

"What? They can't. But we—Officer, we didn't do anything. Honestly. We came around the corner and the fire was already going."

PC Barrows nodded. Did he believe me? I couldn't tell.

"We need to interview you," he said. "But we need to do it with your parents present. Please get in." He pointed to a white car with a yellow and blue stripe parked in the side street.

My legs started to tremble. I was going to be taken to the B&B in a squad car. Gran was going to be awakened so I could be questioned in front of her. I stared at the ground. Why couldn't it just open and swallow me up?

We got into the car. I slumped down in the seat and closed my eyes.

Phil leaned over and said quietly, "We'll say—"

"Girls," the officer warned, "you need to be silent."

I slid away from Phil and hugged the door. In my whole life I had never been so afraid or so mortified. I closed my eyes, hoping that when I opened them I would find I had been having a nightmare.

The car door opened. Someone settled himself in the front seat and closed the door securely. The engine started. I opened my eyes. Then bit my lip. This was real.

"Oh, God," I whispered, "please help."

CHAPTER 18

Friday, 2:00 in the Middle of the Night :(

We went to Phil's apartment first. I had to stay in the kitchen while the officers asked Phil questions in front of her mom. They were in the living room forever! I thought I would explode. Any nanosecond I was going to become a black hole. I tried making mental lists to calm myself. No help there. Suddenly, someone stomped down the hall and slammed a door. I knew it was Phil. What had been said? What was going to happen to her? What was going to happen to me?

The ride to Gran's was like being taken to the principal's office. But four times scarier.

As PC Barrows rang the bell, I looked at my watch. It was 2:30. Aunt Susannah, her green bathrobe flying, answered the door. At first she was all worry and concern. When she learned I had been up on Bruntsfield, my sweet aunt looked decidedly annoyed. I felt terrible.

Briskly, she led us downstairs to Gran's living room and then left to wake up Gran. Aunt Susannah had offered the policemen chairs. PC Barrows sat in the straight-backed chair. The other officer remained standing, leaving the overstuffed chair vacant. I didn't know whether I should sit or stand. Finally because I was suddenly really, really tired, I sat on the couch. But only on the edge.

PC Grantham began asking me questions. How long had I been in Edinburgh? What grade was I in school? Had I done any sightseeing yet? He was nice, really nice. Tears welled up in my eyes and dribbled down my cheeks. I brushed them away, but the more I brushed, the more they flowed.

When Gran came in, she was dressed—sweater, skirt, and shoes. She sat in her usual chair. Aunt Susannah did not sit, but stood behind her. Gran took a deep breath and looked at me evenly. "Now, Elizabeth, what is this all about?"

PC Barrows took out a notebook and pen.

"Mrs. Stewart, Elizabeth is not under caution. We merely want an explanation of tonight's events," PC Grantham said.

"Thank you." Gran turned back to me. "Elizabeth." She nodded for me to begin.

I explained about the fire and how Phil and I had only sounded the alarm. Gran nodded at that. Then the officer asked me to explain why Phil and I had been on the street. Gran stiffened as I told that part of the story. A small smile tugged at Aunt Susannah's lips. She covered her mouth when I said we had been spying on the bakery from Phil's.

PC Barrows cleared his throat. "You said you peeked around the corner. Did you see anyone on the street in front of the dress shop?"

"No, I saw the fire. I did look down the street and across, even the other way. I didn't see anybody close. There was a man, but he was in the next block. Where the street curves."

"Was he coming toward you or away from you?"

"Away."

"Was he running or walking fast?"

"No, he was walking real slow. Except for the fire, the street seemed quiet, asleep."

I thought for a moment—remembering all the noise and frantic running around after we saw the fire. I closed my eyes. It seemed like maybe, maybe there was someone walking away from the fire after the people in the flats came down and tried to put it out. I opened my mouth to say—

PC Grantham's radio squawked from his belt. "Charlie to Charlie Mike 5."

"Excuse me, please," he said, taking the call. "Go ahead, Charlie … Yes ... Right. Thank you." He replaced the radio and turned to me. "Mr. MacLeod has examined the premises of the bakery and reported there is no apparent theft or damage."

I was stunned. We had seen—I had seen a light moving around in the bakery. Why had it been there?

PC Grantham spoke sternly. "You girls put yourselves in danger tonight. The street late at night is no place for unaccompanied young girls. Don't you realize that?"

"Yes," I said in a choked voice.

He turned to Gran and nodded. "Thank you for your cooperation, Mrs. Stewart, Miss Stewart, Elizabeth."

"Thank you, for bringing Elizabeth home," Gran said.

Aunt Susannah led the officers out. Gran leaned back in her chair and sighed heavily.

"I'm sorry, Gran."

"I believe you are, Elizabeth. 'A prudent man foreseeth the evil, and hideth himself: but the simple pass on' — don't restrain themselves — 'and are punished.'"

I sank into myself. "We shouldn't have kept going. We should have stopped."

"Aye. You should have stopped." She put her hand to her lips for a moment and nodded. "You learned a wee hard lesson tonight, did you not?"

"Yes."

"Good. Then we'll say no more about it. Come, give us a hug."

I went to Gran. She wrapped her arms around me and squeezed me tight. "Now off to bed, love."

࿇ ࿇

It felt like I had just crawled into bed when Mags shook me. I was going to tell her to leave me alone, that I had been asleep only a few hours, but I stopped myself. If Mags didn't know about last night, and I had been mouse-quiet when I came in so that I wouldn't wake her, I sure wasn't going to tell her.

I pulled myself from bed. My legs felt like concrete. I kept hoping that any moment there would be a knock on our door and Aunt Susannah would say I didn't have to help this morning. But no such knock came.

Neither Gran nor Aunt Susannah mentioned last night. We served breakfast and then started room cleanings as usual. (Gran made me Alejandra's assistant, which was life-saving. Alejandra was patient with me. Thora would have done me in.) It wasn't until I fell asleep over the lentil soup at lunch that Gran suggested that a wee nap was in order.

I went to my bed without argument.

CHAPTER 19

Friday Afternoon

The next thing I knew, Mags was banging drawers. I half opened my eyes. She was changing into khakis and her brown cashmere pullover. I closed my eyes and heard her running water in the bathroom. She came out brushing her teeth vigorously. I could feel her staring at me.

"Are you going someplace?" I asked sleepily.

"Claire's invited me to the Museum of Scotland. They have a highland harp. So get up and get ready." She went back into the bathroom.

I sat up, dumbfounded. "What? You want ME to go with you?"

I heard her spit into the sink. "No, but it's required," she said, coming back into the room. "I heard about last night, Libby. For the next few days all your extracurricular activities will fall under my supervision."

"I'm being babysat?"

"It appears so."

"That's ugly!"

She nodded firmly. "Correct. But don't worry; I have no intention of hovering." Her face softened. "*Enfant*, last night was pretty stupid. It could have been dangerous."

"Do Mom and Dad know?" I held my breath.

"Gran has decided to let it go."

"Whew!" I flopped back on the bed.

"Will you get going, please?" Mags let her hair out of the scrunchie and shook it loose. "Claire said the museum is connected to the Royal Museum of Scotland. That's the place where they have—"

I bolted out of bed. "You don't have to tell me. That's where they have old telescopes and microscopes." I grinned. Big sisters only THINK they know everything.

Mags and Claire ignored me. Except when Claire treated me like I couldn't blow my own nose. "Elizabeth, dear, hand me your coins and I'll sort out the fare for you." And at the crosswalk, "Careful now, you are crossin' the street." Standing in front of the highland harp, she informed me, "It's a clarsach." Honestly—I could read.

"This harp is said to have belonged to Mary, Queen of Scots." Claire continued, "The one who was beheaded by Elizabeth I."

I touched the screen of the information monitor. "It doesn't say Mary played it. It says Mary GAVE the clarsach to somebody."

"Libby," Mags hissed, "quit acting like an infant. That was rude."

I stuck out my chin. They were being rude to me.

Claire acted like what I said meant less than zero. Though she did rewind her long scarlet neck scarf and it didn't need rewinding. "A harper," she said, "was a valued member of a lord's household. He accompanied the reciter of the poems that told of the darin' deeds of the lord and his ancestors."

"A truly indispensable person," Mags said.

Claire smiled. "It's splendid, is it not? The carving—it's so elegant." She struck a pose as if she were playing it.

I tapped my thigh. I could try to be nice. Maybe it would help. "How long have you been playing the harp?" I asked.

"Since I was six," Claire said.

"Was it hard to learn?"

She glanced at her short, manicured nails. "Aye, some." She smiled at me.

I had scored. I smiled back. I went for two and touched the monitor screen. Music floated around us. "Is that what a clarsach sounds like? It's beautiful, like ... like a running brook."

"It does take you away to a different time, a different place. Margaret, it puts me in mind of the ceilidh tonight. Do you fancy one? A number of our mates will be attending. Jamie MacLeod bein' one."

"Jamie?" Mags gathered her hair in her hands and then let it drop down her back as if to say Jamie being at the ceilidh was zero interest to her. She didn't fool me.

"*Il est vraiment beau, n'est-ce pas?*" Claire said, arching one eyebrow.

"*Qui?*"

Oh, great! NOW they were going to start speaking in French. (I picked out "*n'est-ce pas.*")

Claire pulled Mags off to one side. "Jamie. *Il a un faible pour toi.*" She smiled knowingly.

"*Nous sommes amis, rien d'autre,*" Mags replied, showing off. AND shutting me out. This was too much. Too rude. They were treating me like I wasn't there. Like I was wallpaper.

I hung back, but then, I admit it, just to be mean, I rushed in between them. "Mags, if you and your FRIEND—"

Mags stepped back and put up a hand. She pasted on a smile. "Libby, I'm going to take pity on you. You don't have to stay with us. You may go over to the other part of the museum and wallow in all those old inventions. We'll come and find you in a bit."

"There's a display of clothing from different periods of history on the floor below it. I thought we might take it in," Claire said to Mags. "We can pop up and fetch Elizabeth when we're finished. Here, Elizabeth, let me locate the scientific instruments room for you." She reached for the map of the museum in my hand.

I pulled it away. "That's OK. I CAN read." I opened the brochure, looked at it intently and stomped off.

But I couldn't make sense of the brochure. I searched for an information desk. And found one. The clerk was awfully nice.

Soon I was in this massive white hall that went up three stories. Lots of light and lots of open space—like a courtyard. It had a marble pond too—in the center—and balconies that rimmed the walls. The ceiling was glass. I just stood for a moment looking up, watching the white clouds gather and break apart and gather. Awesome! The telescope exhibit couldn't be any less fantastic.

Following the signs to the Instruments of Science, I clambered up the stairs to the third floor. The exhibit was off the balcony in a separate room.

The Instruments of Science room was a total surprise— dark and shadowy. Light shone only on the microscopes, the telescopes and the written explanations. That was all. I loved it. It felt like a starry night. And there were practically no other people there. I could look at stuff without having to look between people's heads.

Right away I found William Herschel's Newtonian reflecting telescope—the one I had seen in the book. The explanation near the telescope said that Caroline, Herschel's sister, had discovered some comets. I pressed my fingers to the glass. She had probably used a telescope like it.

"Um-m, 1760. In excellent condition, I'd say, for being that old," said a voice behind me. It was Phil.

"Hi," I said. Wow, now I had a friend to be with.

"Your aunt told me you were here. You forgot your telescope at my flat. I brought it 'round," she explained.

Her hair was windblown and her cheeks pink as if she'd been running. "I thought you'd want to know ..." she raised an eyebrow, and then grinned mysteriously.

"Know what?"

"Mr. MacLeod's carrot cakes didn't rise today. Neither did the empire biscuits. Nor the Dundee cakes. Nor the sticky lemon." Her voice got louder with each. "Nor—"

"Sh-h-h. This is like a library," I whispered.

The woman a couple of exhibits away—her face was a huge scold. A man in the next aisle, though, leaned over the case toward us. Weird, he seemed familiar. Had I seen him before? I studied his pudgy body and his round face. No, I decided it was just my imagination. I was turning away when the man took off his knitted hat. He had long hair pulled back into a ponytail. I had seen him before—in the bakery on Tuesday. He was that friend of Mr. MacLeod's.

Phil signaled for me to follow her out on to the balcony. "What I'm tellin' you is the bicarbonate of soda went bad over the night. Mr. MacLeod was furious. You could hear him through the walls."

"Through the walls?"

"Into my mother's shop. She said I had to stay with her today." Phil frowned in disgust, but then brightened. "Which turned out to be a bit of luck since that's how I heard Mr. MacLeod. He was carryin' on. It seems they have this gigantic order every Friday. These two ladies come over from Fife and buy for all their friends. They've done it for years. They come an hour on the train."

"I don't get it. So what if the bicarbonate of soda went bad?"

"It went bad because moisture got into it. If it had rained last night and if the window had been left open. And if the lid of the bicarbonate of soda can had been left open, but none of the above. It had to have been tampered with."

"Then we were right. Someone did get into the bakery last night." I stood up taller.

"Absolutely. Of course, Mr. MacLeod still claims it was a mistake somebody made, but he come into my mother's shop. He asks me a considerable number of questions about what we saw last night."

"Does he want to talk to me?"

"No, I think not. But we've got to pick up our feet. I've been havin' a think on this. Much that's been goin' on, has been goin' on at your granny's B&B. And when I was leavin' it today, Thora was in front of me. She turns up the street to Bruntsfield."

"So?"

"She's the one who lays out the tea at your granny's. I've seen her do it a hundred times."

"Uh?"

"When your granny invites me to stay for a biscuit and a chat. When I deliver stationery and such for Mum. Sometimes, though, I just come around and your granny invites me. She's right nice, your granny."

"Phil!" What was she getting at?

"Right. It's my one failing—I sometimes meander. Anyway, Thora lives with her sister out in Gorgie—it's on another bus line. You catch the bus on a different street. So where is she goin' today? And she's a good baker, so I've heard. She could have made the salty empire biscuits and substituted them. And she comes to work early in the morning, so she could have tampered with the van."

"But why?"

"That I don't know. But we could find out."

"How?"

"Come with me."

"What?"

"I followed Thora to a brasserie just down the street. She's cozy at a table for two. Could be she's meetin' someone. I think we need to see who it is."

I grinned. "Absolutely." We started for the stairs.

Mags' and Claire's voices bounced up from the balcony below. I froze, sucking my cheek. I was being babysat. "I-I can't. I'm—." I broke off and looked away, embarrassed. "I'm supposed to stay with Mags."

"No worries. We'll be back in two ticks—before those two have finished drooling over the Victorian dresses."

"OK." We raced down the stairs to the second floor. "Mags," I said, poking my head into the room with the clothes exhibit. "I'll be right back."

Mags waved absently.

Phil added, "We'll be gettin' something to eat."

Are you lying if the person you are with tells a lie and you don't say otherwise?

—from My Edinburgh Files

CHAPTER 20

Friday Afternoon, Continued!!!

Phil charged down the front steps of the museum. The pigeons left off pecking for food and scattered to the air to get out of her way. She was stopping for nothing. I stopped.

I saw Alejandra coming up the steps, and guilt hit me—big time. Leaving the museum was wrong. I knew it. I turned my head and thought about going back in and rejoining Mags and friend. I didn't. Mistake, big mistake.

Instead I ran, traveling at the speed of light, after Phil. (OK, I exaggerate, but I hoped it was that fast so I could get back to the museum that fast.) Phil led me to a brasserie (a sandwich shop) on the corner. Really, it didn't look like the kind of place a person would choose for a secret rendezvous. In the movies those places were usually shadowy and off of back alleys. The brasserie was on a busy corner. It was well-lit and its walls were practically all window. Secrecy was not possible. You could spot a hamster running around in that place.

With a brief but pointed stare, Phil directed my attention to the back of the shop. A middle-aged woman in boring clothes sat at a small table—Thora. And Phil had been right. She was meeting someone. A large muscular man sat across from her.

"Do you recognize him?" I asked Phil as we strolled casually past the entrance. "Does he work at the bakery?"

Phil pretended to study a poster on the window next to the door. "No, but that means nothing. They're sittin' at the back and this is not her neighborhood.

"Maybe he's her brother. Or her boyfriend?"

"She has no brother. She told me. As to his bein' her boyfriend—look at him. He's tady. And Thora is no beauty. Bad casting that would be."

I got a mental of Thora's face—square with a tiny nose and thin lips. She was no beauty. Phil got that right, but ... "Sometimes guys see what's inside a person," I protested. "My brother Tom has dated—"

"See there, she's handin' him a piece of paper. It's blue and white. I recognize the paper. My mother printed it up for the bakery."

Thora was strict and demanding. She wasn't the friendliest person I had ever met, but would she try to sabotage someone's business?

The man slipped the paper into his jacket pocket too carefully for it to be unimportant. Then he got up.

"He's her accomplice, to be sure," Phil said. "Turn away. He's comin' out."

The man hurried out of the brasserie and crossed the street.

Like a piece of toilet paper stuck to your shoe, we followed him. He got in the queue for a bus. We got in the queue too. I studied him, memorizing what he looked like. A bus pulled up and "our man" got on.

"We need to see where he's goin' with that paper," Phil whispered.

"We can't follow him now."

"Tail him. We're tailing him." Phil corrected already on the steps. "And why not?"

"Because," I whispered back, "because, well—" I searched for a good reason. Something that didn't involve my reminding Phil I was being babysat. That would be way too embarrassing.

Phil was past listening anyway. She dropped some coins into the pay box. "Get on. I paid for you."

I got on the bus.

I told myself that maybe it would only be a short ride. We would see where he was going and find out his name. Maybe. Then we could get back to the museum before Mags and Claire noticed we had been gone. It could happen, I figured. It really could.

If "our man" had intended to go only a few blocks, he would have walked. The Scots like to walk. Unfortunately, I learned that later.

The bus traveled block after block. Minute after precious minute was gobbled up. My hands sweated. I worried if I would get back in time. My hands sweated. Was this man really a villain and what he was going to do next?

Finally, the man, whom Phil dubbed "Compie," got off the bus. He entered a small grocery store and we followed. Phil insisted he would purchase something incriminating. A can of peaches and a carton of orange juice didn't arouse my suspicions.

Next he went into a small bakery.

"We've got him," Phil said triumphantly, and we followed him in.

"I'll have that loaf of whole wheat," the man said.

Phil and I pretended great interest in the pastry case, asking each other which we should buy. Phil pretended to dig in her purse for the money. Breathlessly, we waited and watched for Compie to hand the clerk the piece of paper he gotten from Thora. Maybe he would do it when he paid for the bread. Maybe he would pretend it was a list of other items to purchase.

Compie reached into his trouser pocket and pulled out a black leather coin purse. He handed the counter person some coins. She handed him the bread now in a sack. Compie left.

Phil rushed over to where he had been standing and bent down like she was retying a shoe lace.

"Distract the clerk," she whispered to me. "Move her away from here."

I hurried to the case farthest away.

"Please," I said to the clerk, my voice shaking, "could you tell me what those are?"

The clerk came toward me, wrinkling her mouth as she saw what I was pointing to. "Strawberry tarts."

"Oh, looks good." I smiled weakly. "And what are these?"

"Chocolate éclairs." Her voice was now full of irritation. "Do you want to purchase one?"

"No, thanks," Phil said, yanking me out the door.

"What were you doing? Why did you ask me to—?" I demanded.

Phil scoured the busy street with her eyes. "I thought Compie could have dropped Thora's note to the floor and then with his foot slid it under the counter. The clerk could fetch it there later."

"Is that what Compie did?"

She shook her head. "And now I think he's got away. No, no, there he is." Across the street and half a block down, Compie was standing in front of a store. He pulled a piece of paper from his jacket pocket and studied it. Phil and I ran. We reached the store—a toy store—just after Compie entered. We followed him. The jingling bell on the door announced us. Compie and the store clerk looked at us, their eyes getting squinty. I shuddered. We were found out! They knew we were spying on them. What would they do? What should we do? I got ready to run. But then the men relaxed and casually turned back to their business. We were just kids to them.

"Sorry, mate, I'm sure you want to be closin'," said Compie to the clerk. "But I need to see both of them."

The clerk came out from behind the counter and headed for the shelves.

Meanwhile our man frowned at the paper—the blue and white stationery in his hand. "My girl didn't write down which one to get."

"My girl," I whispered to Phil. "Doesn't that mean girl-friend?"

"Yes, it does," Phil said not the least bit apologetic.

I inched closer to Compie. I recognized the blue and white stationery. It was Gran's B&B stationery, not the bakery's. I scowled at Phil.

The clerk came out from the shelves. He put two boxes of Madeline dolls on the counter.

Compie checked the paper and then the boxes. "I'll take this one, the bigger doll with the change of duds. It's good you had it. In the whole of Edinburgh there's not another. My girl called all the shops. And tomorrow's her niece's birthday."

—*from My Edinburgh Files*

CHAPTER 21

Friday Evening

It was 6:30 when I got back to Gran's. Big trouble. Oh, why had I gone with Phil? Mags pounced on me as I tore past the staircase on my way to the kitchen.

"Where have you been?" she shouted from the landing. "You said you were going to the coffee shop in the museum."

"I never said that."

"You did. And now I'm in trouble."

"Girls," Gran said sternly, coming from the kitchen. "Stop the shouting. My guests have no need to hear this. Elizabeth, follow me downstairs. Margaret, you come as well."

I swallowed hard. "Yes, Gran."

In her living room, Gran, ignoring her comfortable overstuffed chair, marched straight to the mantel. There she turned and motioned for me to take a seat on the couch.

I bit my lip. This was going to be ugly. I sidled toward the couch and sat. Mags dropped into the overstuffed chair and casually crossed her legs. After she glanced at Gran, she un-crossed them. I frowned. My sister still looked smug.

"Margaret, you are not 'in trouble.'" Gran made air quotes.

I stared. I didn't think grandmothers did that.

"You are not at fault." Gran continued, looking at Mags steadily. "Elizabeth made her own decision. And, Elizabeth, were you not told that you were under your sister's guardianship?"

"Yes, Gran, I was told."

"And did you obey?"

"No, Gran."

"Did you lie to your sister?"

I shifted uncomfortably. "I said I would be right back and I meant to. Only..."

"Did you lie?"

"Yes, Gran, I guess I did."

Gran nodded and sat down next to me on the couch. "Elizabeth, you frightened your sister. And put her in an awkward position."

"I-I wasn't thinking, Gran. I'm sorry. I'm sorry, Mags.

Mags softened. "I forgive you. But," Mags leaned forward, "where were you? Where did you go?"

I pulled at my hair, embarrassed. I didn't want to tell them. It all seemed so childish now. So silly. "Phil was desperate to show me something and I got caught up in it and—" I looked at the floor.

"What did she want you to see?" Mags asked.

I glared at her. Why did she have to be so nosey? I traced the rose on Gran's rug with the toe of my shoe. "Thora and her boyfriend, as it turned out."

"Thora has a boyfriend?!"

Wow! I knew something that Mags didn't. "Yeah, and he's good-looking," I added.

"Where did you see him?"

"At the brasserie near the museum."

"Girls—"

Mags smirked. "I'll bet Thora gave it to you two when she caught you spying on her."

I shuddered. She would have. "She didn't see us. I don't want to talk about it anymore. Please."

"Margaret," Gran warned. "Elizabeth, it's good to take an interest in others. But you and Philippa crossed the line into being busybodies."

"I see that, Gran."

Gran shook her head and sighed. "Philippa is a lovely girl, full of spirit and imagination. I like her, but she can be ... she can be highly persuasive. I think you need to consider your friendship with her prayerfully. God does not want you led astray."

I nodded.

Gran put a hand on my shoulder. "Elizabeth, it's no easy adjusting to a new place and making new friends, I well know. But I'm confident you will do fine, my girl." She stood and smiled.

It was good of her to say so. From where I saw it, I was failing miserably.

"Let's see what dinner is left for you," she said, leaving the room.

"*Enfant*, Gran didn't say it, but she was pretty worried about you."

I opened my mouth to jump on my sister for calling me an infant but let it pass. I deserved the name. "Is Gran going to send me to Mom and Dad?"

Mags shook her head slowly. "I doubt it. No, I don't think she will. But give her a break and try not to get into any more trouble. At least for a while." She glanced at her watch. "Oops, got to go."

I followed Mags into the stairwell. "Where are you going?"

"The ceilidh. Claire invited me. Remember?"

I remembered. So I should have let it go, but I didn't. "Please, Mags, may I go with you?" I asked, catching up with her.

Mags shook her head slightly.

"I wouldn't be a problem. Honest, Mags. I promise. Please. It's really hard being alone."

Mags sighed.

"And, Mags, think of it. It would be educational for me. Mom and Dad would be so pleased with you. You know, nurturing my Scottish roots and all."

Mags rolled her eyes.

"OK," I persisted as we climbed the main staircase to our room. "Gran put you in charge of me, and where you go, I go. And, Mags, we messed up today. OK, I messed up. But tonight would give me a chance to redeem myself. Please,

Mags. And it would show Gran what great leadership qualities you have." I grinned.

"Nice try," Mags said, unlocking the door to our room. "I particularly like the leadership part. But I can't take you. It would be, you see, a bit awkward for me."

"A bit awkward for YOU?"

"Yes, Claire could —"

"Mags, that's all you care about — you! You're mean and selfish. I wish you'd never come."

She blinked, hurt crossing her face. She turned and reached for the long (I had never seen it before), gorgeous black scarf on her bed and wound it stylishly around her neck. "So I guess you'll be happy I'm not sleeping here tonight."

"What? Where are you sleeping?"

Mags grabbed her leather jacket and her pack back from her bed. "Claire's. See you in the morning. Don't forget to set the alarm." She left.

I shut the door — hard.

CHAPTER 22

Friday Night, Continued

From: Libby Carlsen
Subject: mad at Mags
To: Tom Carlsen <carlsenT@christiancom.net>

Tom, you wanted the news.

THE NEWS: For dinner Gran made steak and kidney pie and Mags is a pig. OK, no name-calling, but she went out with her new BFF and didn't let me go with. Since we got here she's always doing that. I hate it. She acts like I'm a sub-atomic particle, less than a subatomic particle.

And remember Phil, the girl I e-mailed you about? Well, I got into trouble again today because of her. Gran hinted we shouldn't be friends. Who am I going to be friends with?

Well, maybe I won't need friends here. Tom, I think Gran might not let me stay. She's probably wishing she had never said yes to Mom. She's probably thinking how she can get out of it and send me to Mom and Dad in Ecuador. Major humiliation!

And this is weird—I don't want to go. I kind of like it here. It's interesting and exciting and scary. Sometimes in the same nanosecond. Tom, I wish you were here.

Love, Libby

I sent the message and was halfway through one to Krissy when a message came in.

From: Tom Carlsen
Subject: Love ya
To: Libby Carlsen<libby1@shepherd-house.serve.co.uk>

Lillibet,

Wish i were there too. Except then i wouldn't be going camping this afternoon.

This afternoon? What was my brother talking about? It was nighttime. Oh, right. Different time zone. My brother and I weren't even living in the same time of day. How could I think he would understand what was happening here? I wanted to cry. I was so alone. I frowned at the monitor and read.

About Mags—you're not a subatomic particle and she doesn't think so either. She loves you. She just thinks about Mags too much sometimes. But then we all do SOMETIMES. Except maybe me. I'm the perfect one.

"Yeah, right, Tom." I chuckled and then tapped the desk. I was furious with Mags because she was only thinking about herself. She was being mean and selfish. Majorly. But when I left the museum with Phil, I had only been thinking about me. I continued reading —

> About Gran—Stop worrying! She was a pastor's wife. Remember? They're used to challenges. You would have to get into mega trouble before she would kick you out. I can't imagine you getting into that much trouble.
>
> About Phil—she sounds fun, but maybe you need to expand your sights. Are there other kids you could hang with? Come on; give other Scots a chance to know your stunning personality. I also recommend someone else. Check Deuteronomy 31:6.
>
> GTR. Mom and Dad are off on some training retreat and I have been assigned the watering of the potted plants and fruit trees. Hey, I wish you were here. Then you could do it instead of me. :)
>
> LY, Tom

Deuteronomy 31:6. I wrote it on my hand and glanced up. On a shelf above the monitor was a large black book. On its spine in gold letters was Holy Bible. I took it down and found the verse. (OK, I didn't find it right away. I finally thought to check the Table of Contents.)

"... he will not fail thee nor forsake thee," the Scripture said.

"Fine, Tom, nice verse. But I want a friend." I flopped back in the chair, disappointed. Having nothing else to do, I Googled "forsake." It meant "abandon." I crossed my arms on the desk next to the keyboard and dropped my head onto my arms. I sighed. "God, I need a friend, please," I whispered. I don't know where the idea came from, but I decided to write a letter to God.

> *Dear God,*
>
> *Things are not good, but you already know that. God, I don't know what to do about Phil.*
>
> *REASONS THAT I WANT TO BE FRIENDS*
> > *Nice to me.*
> > *Fun.*
> > *Knows how to get around here and I don't.*
> > *Likes me.*
> > *My only friend here. Judging from how I went over with Claire, Phil may be the only friend I'll make.*
>
> *REASONS WHY I SHOULDN'T HANG WITH HER*
> > *She acts without thinking, I think.*
> > *She says things without thinking.*
> > *The trouble I get into when I'm with her.*
>
> *God, what should I do? Can you help me? How?*
>
> *Respectfully,*
> *Libby*

I waited. I hoped I would hear something. That I would get an idea in my head and it would be from God. I thought just maybe there would be a knock on the door and that would be from God. Nothing. I trudged up to my room and washed my hair.

"He will not fail thee," kept running through my head. It was like some CD on replay. "But, God," I said, squeezing water from my hair, "you have failed me. I am so alone."

I blow dried my hair, dragged myself into my nightgown, thought about reading, but slid under the covers   instead. I shut my eyes.

CHAPTER 23

Saturday, 1:25 in the Middle of the Night!!!

When I opened my eyes again, the room was inky black. Outside a fierce wind was blowing. It rattled and banged the windows like in some horror movie. I looked at the clock—1:25. Four hours, thirteen minutes until daylight. I sat up and hugged my knees. I was way past believing in monsters in the closet, but still ... I switched on the light.

My telescope case lay on the floor beside my bed. A little star-gazing might make me feel better, I decided. I hopped out of bed and began setting up.

By the time I was ready to turn off the lamp on the nightstand, I was excited. (Looking at the night sky is seriously awesome!!) I pulled back the drapes and happily shoved the window up all the way. I got blasted—the air was cold, freezing. Icicle time. I felt for my robe at the bottom of my bed. It wasn't there. Grumbling, I yanked at the sleeves of my nightgown and checked out the sky. And then I couldn't believe it—no stars! Not a one. Only clouds, the color of lead.

"God, this is not fair," I complained, plopping down on my bed and pulling the quilt around me. "Couldn't you even let me have a star for a friend? It's not fair at all. Phil was right. You are on vacation."

Tom's verse played in my brain again, though I didn't invite it. And now I remembered Gran had also read those same words that morning during Bible reading. "What is this?" I sighed. "OK, OK, maybe I do get it. Honestly, though, God, I don't feel that you are here. Not at all." The wind gusted, smacking the trees and whistling around my window. I huddled into the quilt. "But please, God, please, be here with me."

A dog barked ferociously. Suddenly, Gran's porch light jumped on, spilling light into the parking lot. The hair on my arms stood on end. Someone must be down there to make the light come on. It was on a motion sensor. I went to the window and stared out, but didn't see anyone. Had the gate clanged? No. I hadn't heard footsteps or voices either.

"The cat." I grinned. "Sunshine, it's you, right? You are leaving us a giftee. That's why the light went on."

The porch light went off.

Then I heard them. Quick, hard steps coming from Gran's car park. A voice, hushed but angry, said something. I couldn't make it out. I leaned way out the window, trying to hear, trying to see who was in the darkness. There were more footsteps, but these were different. The person wore sandals. I heard the slap-slap of them.

From way down the block, voices, loud and happy, drifted up. People were coming up the street.

In the car park below, a man whispered sharply. Immediately the person wearing sandals ran, but away from the house. Wood scraped along stone and a gate creaked. Someone was pushing open the gate along the back wall. Why? Almost nobody used that back gate or the pathway that lay alongside the church.

I grabbed the flashlight on the nightstand and bolted from the room and down the stairs. Just as I reached the bottom step, the house went pitch black. Power failure. Everything outside was pitch black too. For a moment I stood, fear gluing my feet to the carpet. "Come on," I muttered and switched on my flash light.

As soon as I cracked open the B&B's front door, I heard the footsteps again. The someone in the hard-soled shoes was running toward the back wall. Light from a flashlight hit the back gate. Again the gate scraped across stone. Then the hard-soled shoes pounded on the church path. He was running, getting away, and no one had seen him. I rushed past the cars and the van and hid behind Gran's tall wooden gate. That's when it decided to rain. Big fat drops.

Somewhere down the church path, a metal gate clanged and a woman's voice, hushed and angry, said something. I heard it, but I couldn't understand it. She hadn't spoken in English. I thrust my head out from behind the gate.

In their flashlights I made out a man, but only from the waist down. As he reached the woman, their beams of light went toward Bruntsfield.

I decided to follow them—well, partway. I figured I could run down the path, stop before the end of the church, and peek around its corner. I could get a better look at them maybe.

By the time I got to the end of the church, it was pouring. Cold little rivers ran down my face and legs. Wet nightgown clung to my back and my arms, chilling me to ice cube status. I started to shake. "F-f-forget the c-c-cold. J-j-ust find out who they are. Find-d out ... find out." I ordered.

I sucked in a breath—the air was glacial—and shoved my head around the corner. And then, I couldn't help it—I sneezed.

The light from one of their flashlights swung around. The light started toward me. For an eternity I was a deer in the lights of an oncoming car. My heart pounded, my breath stopped, and I was rooted to the ground. Then I ran. My feet slid through mud and stumbled over rocks— no matter. I kept running.

I didn't stop until I reached Gran's front steps. The outside door was still open. I scooted into the lobby and shut the door behind me. Pressing my back against the door, I waited for the sound of footsteps. After a few moments I noticed that I still had my flashlight on. I turned it off and cracked open the door. There was nothing in the dark but the dark. I was going to be fine.

"OK, OK now think," I told myself, rubbing my arms and jumping about to keep from freezing. "Think about ... a man and a woman ... they—they were here. They were sneaking around. Why? Did—did they do something to the van? Did they leave a tool—with fingerprints maybe?"

I turned on my flashlight and rushed to the van. I circled it. Nothing on the ground. Annoyed, I shoved my wet hair out of my face and stared at the van. Something looked wrong. What was it? I walked slowly around to the front of the van. Then I got it. Like the Leaning Tower of Pisa, the van was listing to one side. Two of the tires on its left side were flat.

I ran up the steps, into the lobby and to Gran's inside door. I stopped and bit my lip. The door—it was probably locked. I tried the handle. Locked up good!!! I wanted to scream. Instead I just stood there dripping puddles onto Gran's tiles and peering through the glass into the black cavern that was her hallway. I frowned. Nobody was going to come. Not by my just wishing it. I had to do something. I had to ring the bell.

For the second night in a row, Aunt Susannah came to the door and in her bathrobe. I could tell, even with only the light from our flashlights, that she wasn't happy.

CHAPTER 24

Saturday, 2:30 in the Middle of the Night

I was upstairs in my room when the police arrived. (Aunt Susannah had sent me there to put on something dry.) I was surprised—about the police being called. Someone had only let the air out of the van's tires. Why would the police come for something like that?

Aunt Susannah came to my room just as I was trying to squeeze water from my wet hair. "The police are wantin' to interview you next," she said. I grabbed my lighted flashlight and followed her into the pitch-dark hallway. Below us a light moved slowly up the staircase—Mr. Brown trudging back up to his room. He had slippers on his feet and I saw his pajama top poking out from under his suit jacket.

"So sorry about all this," Aunt Susannah said as we passed him.

"It's not your fault," he said.

"What did he mean?" I whispered to her.

"His rental car as well," she said quietly.

"So sorry to disturb your sleep," Aunt Susannah said to a couple who came out of their room. "Just a bit of vandalism. It's bein' managed."

Outside the motor of the bakery van kicked over and roared. Aunt Susannah sighed with relief I thought.

"I could do with a biscuit or two. How about you?" she asked as we reached the bottom of the staircase.

"Yes, thank you."

She squeezed my shoulder. "I'll be back with a plate in two ticks."

I shut off my flashlight and slipped in the open door of Gran's breakfast room. The room was lit up with candles on a couple of the tables and on the mantelpiece. The shadows and the flickering candles made the room seem kind of spooky. It also felt kind of exciting, especially when I saw PC Grantham sitting with the Englishman at one of the candlelit tables. PC Grantham had his notebook out and was writing things down. I wondered what the Englishman had told him. Had he seen something or heard something? I noticed then that, unlike Mr. Brown, the Englishman was wearing a sweater and slacks. Was he one of the people I heard coming up the street just before the lights went out?

Gran was standing in front of the window and looking out. She also wore everyday clothes, but I was pretty sure she had put them on just as she had put on a sweater and skirt when the police and I came the night before. It was what she did. That was Gran. Had it only been the night before? I slipped between the tables and walked over to Gran. She seemed far away. I touched her arm. Turning to me, she smiled softly and stroked my still wet hair. Then she wrapped her arms around and hugged me tightly—a little more tightly than usual.

"Mrs. Stewart, we are ready for you and Elizabeth," PC Barrows said, coming up to us. Gran turned. PC Barrows, his hat and slicker glistening with rain, nodded. He directed us to the table where PC Grantham was sitting with his notebook, and Gran and I sat down. I told them what I had heard. And what I had seen, which was almost nothing. They thanked me for my report and left.

The house and the street returned to quiet. The rain turned to mist. And almost as if a signal had been given, the lights popped on.

"Gran, I don't get it," I said, blowing out a candle. Why did you call the police? Did you think that the people who let the air out of the tires had maybe also broken the van?"

"Elizabeth, they didn't let the air out. They slashed the tires."

"They slashed them? They had a knife?" I started to shake. "Gran, I-I ..."

Gran put an arm across my shoulder. "Come now. We need some tea. Or maybe cocoa?" She led me out of the breakfast room toward the kitchen. Her lips moved silently. I wondered if she was angry, but she didn't look angry. Then I heard her say softly, "Amen." Tears sprang to my eyes.

"Thank you, God, that they didn't hurt me," I whispered.

After I finished my cup of cocoa, Gran sent me to bed. I was happy to go. Dead doesn't half tell you how I felt.

But in bed I tossed and turned. My mind was just too full. It was like when I was little and my mom would say, "Clean your room." I would take everything off the shelves and pile it all in the middle of the room. It made a huge mess. It would take me forever to put it all away.

Now I had a huge mess in my mind. And I couldn't find a shelf for anything. I kept trying, though. Finally I gave up and slept. I had this weird dream about exploding puzzle pieces that morphed into exploding stars.

Either the vacuum running in the next room or my stomach growling woke me up. Half-asleep, I couldn't decide which. Both were really noisy. Suddenly I vaulted into awake mode. What time was it if the vacuum was running? I jumped out of bed in a panic. Had I slept through my alarm? Vaguely I remembered Mags standing over me and Aunt Susannah telling her to let me sleep.

After pulling on jeans and a blue sweater, I headed for the kitchen. Food first, I figured.

"Good morning, dear," Aunt Susannah said as I entered. "Here," she said, handing me two steaming mugs. I sniffed. One smelled of coffee and the other of cocoa. "Take these, please, to Mr. MacLeod and Malcolm in the car park. And when you return, I'll have your porridge ready for you. Or would you rather eggs and bacon?"

"All, please?"

Aunt Susannah grinned. "Right."

Malcolm and Mr. MacLeod had already changed one of the van tires. They were working on the second when

I handed them the mugs. Thanking me, they took them, sipped and went back to work. Mr. MacLeod worked the jack. Then Malcolm twisted off the nuts.

I shifted from one foot to the other and hoped they would talk to me. I wanted to know what they thought was going on. I needed more pieces of the puzzle. Stuff was happening—some of it to me—and not good stuff.

I searched my mind for something to say. "I didn't know vans had two spare tires."

"They don't," Malcolm said angrily. "Dad had to ring the tyre fitter to have one brought around."

I nodded. "I felt terrible when I saw all this last night. Who would do such a thing? I wish I had seen them."

Malcolm's jaw tightened.

"Thank you for reportin' it," Mr. MacLeod said.

I smiled and waited. After a few moments I realized nothing more was going to be said. I turned to leave. A flash of orange caught my attention. Sunshine was stalking something in the flower bed that edged the wall. A bird?

"Sunshine," I called. "Sunshine come here. Come here, kitty, kitty."

She stopped. Her ears flicked, but then she ignored me.

"Sunshine, we really don't need any giftees."

She pawed at a large nest among the plants. I rushed over, chasing her away. Fortunately, the nest was empty. "I've never seen such a large nest." I said.

"It's a dray," Malcolm said, coming up behind me. "A squirrel's nest. The squirrels build them in the trees. They build them sturdy, see?"

I squatted to get a closer look.

"But in the wind last night this one got knocked out." He lifted it up with the toe of his shoe.

I gasped. There beneath the nest was a pocketknife with the blade still out. I pushed the nest aside. (I could wash my hands later.) "Look!" I shrieked. I didn't need to say that. Malcolm had squatted down immediately.

"No," he said, "can't be."

"Don't touch it," I ordered. "They'll want to fingerprint— the police I mean. They'll want to—" I ran toward the house.

"Da," Malcolm said, "you'd best have a look at this."

Something in his voice made me stop and turn back.

Aunt Susannah came up behind me. "Your breakfast—"

I broke in. "The knife, we found the knife. There." I pointed.

Aunt Susannah hurried to where Malcolm and Mr. MacLeod were standing over the knife as if it were a dead body. Curious, I followed her.

"What's wrong, Jock?" Aunt Susannah asked. She touched his arm. "What's wrong?"

He shook her off. His beard wobbled, then his jaw set tight. "It's Jamie's knife," he said angrily. "Jamie's."

"No. Are you sure?" she asked.

CHAPTER 25

Saturday Morning

Mr. MacLeod wanted to pocket the knife. This was a matter between himself and his son, he insisted. Aunt Susannah disagreed. The tires of her guests had been slashed as well. The police would be informed.

I expected her to ask me to stand guard over the knife, but she didn't. She went into the house and told me to come too. Mr. MacLeod would be trusted apparently.

In the kitchen I picked at my eggs while Aunt Susannah talked on the phone to the police. I had just popped a piece of bacon into my mouth when Mags came in.

"There you are, Libby. Could you up the tempo? Rachmaninoff it? You're supposed to be helping—"

"Sh-h-h." I put a finger to my lips and nodded toward Aunt Susannah.

"What's going on?" Mags whispered to me.

"I found the knife. Aunt Susannah is telling the police. And, Mags, the knife belongs—Malcolm says it does—to his brother Jamie. It looks like Jamie—"

Mags stepped back, horrified. "But Jamie, he wouldn't. True, he's angry with his father. His father is forcing him to come into the business and he wants no part of it. But Jamie wouldn't do anything to hurt the bakery. I just know he wouldn't. He wouldn't do anything like that."

I got up and rinsed off my dishes. "Sorry, Mags, but this is one time you're wrong." Mags raised her head and looked down her nose at me. It didn't work like it usually did. I didn't cave in. That startled me. Coolly I left. Mags followed me out into the hall.

"I'm not wrong," Mags insisted. "I know I'm not. He wouldn't do anything like that."

"Well, it's his knife. It has the 'M' scratched on it."

"He could have lost it," Mags fired back.

"Yeah, right."

Mags straightened. "He isn't the one you saw last night, is he?"

"I didn't really see anyone. I only saw—what do you call it when the light is behind someone and you only see their shape and its all in black?

"Silhouette."

"Yeah, silhouette. That's all I saw. Oh, and I heard them—a man and a woman."

"What time?"

"Just before two o'clock."

129

"Then it wasn't Jamie," she said firmly. She shuddered and pulled me into the stairwell. "I was with Jamie at two," she said quietly.

I gasped. "But I thought you were supposed to be with Claire. Mags, you're going to get grounded."

Mags hung her head. "Yeah, I deserve it, I suppose. It was stupid. We went to this club—all of us. The music was description-defying fabulous, incredible. An electric violinist. She was amazing!" Mags eyes glazed over.

She did that about music. Usually I just waited for her to come back to earth. But not that time. "Mags," I demanded.

She blinked. "Oh, yeah. Around midnight Claire and the others decided to leave. Jamie and I stayed—just another half hour or so. Well, maybe a little more. But then I lost my watch—"

"You lost Mom's watch?!" I couldn't believe it. And she thought I would lose it!!!

"Don't stress. We found it. We went back to the club and found it. It took a while, but we found it. But by that time, the buses had stopped running. We had to walk. And the club was clear across town. And in the rain. It was awful. I think I ruined my jacket. We didn't get to Claire's until almost three. So it couldn't have been Jamie."

"What are you doing?" I asked. She was going downstairs to Gran's and Aunt Susannah's apartment.

"I think Gran is down there. I need to tell her what I did last night and that it couldn't have been Jamie who slashed the tires."

A car motor turned over. I ran to the front door. The van was pulling out through the street gate. Malcolm stood by the gate, ready to close it.

"Stop," I shouted and ran around the front of the van to the driver's side. "Mr. MacLeod, Jamie didn't slash the tires. Mags, my sister, said he was with her. They were at a club across town."

Mr. MacLeod slumped back against the seat. He wiped his face with his big hand and sighed. "Thank you, lassie. Thank you, for tellin' me."

"Da, may I walk up to the shop?" Malcolm asked.

Mr. MacLeod looked puzzled, then nodded and drove away.

"I want to know," Malcolm said, "what you heard last night and what you saw. I also want to know what you and Pippa saw the night before."

"Why? You said Phil was crazy and a nosey parker."

Malcolm frowned and crossed his arms across his chest. "Someone is tryin' to hurt my father's business and I want to know who."

"OK, but I want to help you. A lot of this stuff keeps happening to me. Besides, it seems like we ought to pool our info."

Malcolm sucked his cheek as if he were considering this. Then he nodded. "May I use your phone?"

"I guess. Who are you going to call?"

He smiled sheepishly. "Miss Nosey Parker."

CHAPTER 26

Saturday Morning, 10:30

Phil showed up at Gran's in a too-big raincoat and a beret. "Well ...?" she asked, strutting like a model in front of Malcolm and me as we sat on the stairs in Gran's hallway. "OK, not splendid." She frowned. "If I'd more time, I could have gotten real detective clothes—trench coat and slouch hat. The brown raincoat, Mum's, was the best I could do on ten minutes' notice. If you're goin' to sleuth, you have to dress the part."

Mags stormed into the hallway from the breakfast room where she had been wiping tables. "You're pathetic. This is not a play or a game," she said hotly. "This is serious."

"Margaret." Malcolm glanced at his watch and frowned. "I beg pardon, but I've not the time for arguin'. I'm needed at the shop. It matters to me no what she wears."

Mags opened her mouth and then surprisingly shut it.

We all went into the breakfast room and took seats around the table closest to the window.

"Why the notepad and pen?" Phil asked, pointing to the notebook and pen I laid on the table. "The minutes of the last meeting of Clues, Inc. Wait. What a splendid name for—"

"Will you stop?!!" Mags broke in, glowering at her from across the table. My sister was on the edge. She could erupt at any moment.

"The paper and pen are because I like to write things down when I'm trying to figure something out. It helps me to think." I swallowed and looked down, embarrassed.

"Excellent," Malcolm said. "Maybe we should all write, but what should we write?" He wrinkled his forehead. "I know. Libby, write what you saw and heard last night. And Pippa, write what you saw the night before. And I shall write about—"

"Every mysterious occurrence at the bakery," said Pippa, a.k.a. Phil.

"And just what would that be?" Malcolm challenged her.

"The wrong order." she said knowingly.

"And how did you come by that information?"

"Your father had to fax the company his disagreement with them." Phil smoothed the collar of her coat and smiled smugly. "Sometimes havin' a mum who runs a copy shop is useful."

Mags chuckled. "I'll go get some pens."

I ripped out some sheets of paper and passed them to Malcolm and Phil. I started writing down what happened last night.

When Mags returned, I had written only a few sentences. It was slow work. The others began writing, except Mags. She fiddled with the clasp on her—Mom's—watch. Then she put her head on the table and closed her eyes. I wondered what kind of punishment Gran had given her for what she did last night.

"This is laborious. Might there not be a faster way?" Phil complained.

"Maybe we could just list things?" I offered.

"I was just thinking that, " Mags said.

I rolled my eyes.

"I was," she insisted. "We need to make a list of 'what.' What happened and when."

Phil bounced in her chair. "Yes. And followin' that, we should make a list of 'who'—who might want to harm MacLeod's."

Malcolm sucked the end of the pen. He nodded. "Lists are good." He drew a line through the paragraph he had written, and a couple spaces down he wrote, "What happened."

"We need to put down all the unusual things that have happened, say, for the last week," Mags said.

We made a list and then recopied it so the events were in the order that they happened.

> EVENTS
>> the van broke down
>> the van broke down again

an order wasn't placed
a wrong order was placed
a light was seen in the bakery
a rubbish fire happened outside the bakery
the van tires were slashed

We looked over the list. We crossed off 'an order wasn't placed' because Jamie had admitted he forgot.

"Anything else?" Mags asked.

"Yes," I said, reading the list again, "those awful cookies Gran served for tea."

"Right." Malcolm added it to the list. "And the bakery goods that didn't rise." He added that also.

Mags stretched her hands over her head. "Except for the van breaking down the first time, everything has happened since we arrived. Good thing I don't know anything about auto mechanics, or people might be suspecting me."

"You don't know anything about baking either, but in the case of those cookies that would have helped," I said.

"Little sister!" Mags exclaimed. Then she laughed.

Phil pulled the list toward her and read. "It's got to be an inside job," she said after a moment.

Malcolm raised a hand in protest. "Please, no cousin from the Isles. My father's no feudin' with any of the family."

"Fine," Phil said irritably. "But someone got inside the shop the other night."

"And somebody," I said, "must have done something to the dough to make those cookies that Gran bought taste so awful."

"It sounds like we're at a 'who' list," Mags said.

CHAPTER 27

Saturday Morning, 10:57

I sucked my lower lip. "Malcolm, I'm sorry to ask, but who works at the bakery? Would one of them want to cause trouble? We have to consider all the possibilities."

"Aye, I grasp that, but—" He shook his head. "No one who works for m'dad would cause trouble. Besides, no one would want to jeopardize their job, would they? Wilma and Ellie, who work the counter, both need their wages. As do Mike and Dennis, our bakers."

"And nobody is new." Phil frowned and shook her head. "Too bad!! It just reeks of an inside job. You know, someone got the job just so he could damage things."

Malcolm threw his head back and stared at the ceiling.

"Well, I've seen it happen in films," Phil protested. "Wait! Sometimes people get hired for a job a long time before they do damage. They work there, actin' like model employees, and then one day someone rings them. It is time, they are told, for them to become a saboteur. Then—"

Mags dropped her head to the table dramatically. I scratched an "X" on the paper so I wouldn't say something rude.

"I work with these people," Malcolm said between gritted teeth. "I know them. They have worked with m'dad for a long time."

"Yes, as I said a long time can go by before--But, wait. Oh, oh, Mike has not been with your dad all that long. He's rather new."

Mags lifted her head. "How new? When did he start?"

"Three months ago," Malcolm said. "And he needs his pay." He glared at Phil.

She tossed her head defiantly, but said nothing.

We sagged into our elbows, frustrated. Suddenly I had an idea. I sat up straight. "Did your dad hire Mike because he needed more workers?"

Phil bounced on her chair. "No," she said. "Mr. MacLeod sacked Ian—fired him. Ian would want revenge. He didn't think sackin' him was fair. He was quite loud about it. I heard it through the walls."

"Why didn't Ian think it was fair?" I asked Malcolm.

"Because Mr. MacLeod fired him for drinking," Phil interjected.

Malcolm shook his head. "I must remind m'dad about the thinness of the walls. And, aye, he did fire him for drinking," Malcolm said, "but Ian right away got another job. I don't—"

Phil cut him off. "He's the one."

"But how did he get into the shop the other night?" I asked.

Malcolm sighed. "Ian did have a key. He was the first baker in the morning. But I know m'dad got it back when he sacked him."

"He had a duplicate made, to be sure." Phil said with an it-is-settled nod.

"OK, how are we going to expose him?" Mags asked.

"Wait, Mags," I said, shaking my head. "This sounds too obvious." (In science you learn not to jump at the first possibility. I had gone on a wild goose chase with Phil the other day. I wasn't going on another.) "Maybe somebody else had a key too."

Malcolm pushed his hair back and squinted like people do when they're thinking. He frowned. "Nunzio had a key. He watched the shop whilst we were up at Skye for my granddad's funeral."

"Nunzio?" Phil asked.

I got a chill. "Nunzio—he's Italian, isn't he?"

"Who's Nunzio?" Phil asked again.

"Yes, he's Italian," Malcolm said.

"I remember something," I said. "Last night, the girl who was with the guy who slashed the tires, I heard her speak. She said something in a foreign language. It could have been Italian."

Impatiently Mags pulled off her scrunchie and redid her ponytail. "I don't get it. Why would this Nunzio person want to sabotage the bakery?"

"Who is he?" Phil demanded.

"He owns The Bread Shop and he wouldn't sabotage us," Malcolm said, his eyes flashing. "He's a friend. M'dad was his apprentice and worked in his shop before we opened ours."

"He's a competitor," Phil said, rapping her pencil on the table.

"He's no competitor. There's a rivalry, aye, but it's between friends," Malcolm protested. "I tell you he's a pal."

"Malcolm, this is the same man who came here the other morning, the man with the bread, right?" I asked.

"Aye, he's the one."

"Mustache, gray hair, shorter than your dad and heavier." I thought about the silhouette of the man I saw leaving the fire scene. Then I thought about the man I had seen running down the path last night. Neither man had been tall and thin, but did either of them look like Nunzio? Maybe. "Does Nunzio have a daughter?"

"No, he has no children."

"He has a wife, though?"

Malcolm set his jaw. "Nunzio and his wife are both friends. They would no want to harm us."

I bit my lip, but then said it anyway. "Nunzio seemed awfully friendly with the Browns. And Mr. Brown is a buyer at the trade show. Are your dad and Nunzio competing for Mr. Brown's business?"

Malcolm sighed.

Phil wrote "Who" on her paper. Underneath it she wrote "Ian." Below that she wrote "Nunzio." She wrote again but covered it with her hand. She nudged me and uncovered it. She grinned. She had written "feuding cousin from Skye."

I rolled my eyes.

Mags glanced over. Her eyes narrowed to slits. "Could we be serious?" she said irritably. (My sister is not the most fun person when she hasn't had much sleep.) She turned to Malcolm. "Jamie mentioned the trade show that opens tomorrow. What happens if your father gets some contracts from it?"

"We expand."

Mags raised an eyebrow. "The store owners on either side would not be happy about that. Maybe one of them—"

"Are you accusing my mother of—" Phil said hotly.

"Your mother's shop is on one side of the bakery? Oh, yes, the thin walls. Sorry," Mags said.

Phil, her eyes now narrowed to slits, leaned across the table toward Mags. "Well, I won't have you even SPECULATING about it."

"She's not; we're not," I said. "Besides your mother was home the night of the trash fire."

"Thank you very much for THAT, I think," Phil said, turning away in a huff.

Malcolm pushed his hair back from his eyes. "I suppose we must consider Violet Murdock, the dress shop owner. But somebody tampered with the van. Ms. Murdock wouldn't know how to do that, would she?"

"You mean because she's a woman?" Mags asked. Mags and Phil both looked at Malcolm as if he had better choose his next words very carefully.

"It doesn't matter. She had an accomplice," I said. "I saw a man running away. But how would she get into the shop the other night? Did she have a key?"

"No," Malcolm said. "So that eliminates her."

"Wrong," Phil said. "Some of the shops were bigger at one time. In my mother's shop there's a door into the fishmonger's that's been nailed shut."

"Maybe Phil should check out Ms. Murdock's store," I said.

The door opened and Aunt Susannah stood in the doorway. "This is an interesting gatherin'. Comin' up with answers, I hope."

"More questions," I said.

She shook her head. "It's puzzling, but I'm afraid the solution will have to wait a bit. Thora and Alejandra need help if they're to finish cleanin' the rooms."

"We're at a stoppin' place," Malcolm said.

Aunt Susannah left. Mags dragged herself to her feet and moved toward the door.

"I'll check out Ms. Murdock," Phil said.

I studied the list of suspects. "Malcolm, I think we need to know if Nunzio returned the key. And what do we do about Ian?"

"Does he have an alibi for last night and the night before?" Mags asked.

"Good thought. If he is workin' the graveyard shift, he could no be here. I'll find out where he is workin' from m'dad."

"It might tell us something if we knew when Jamie lost his knife," Mags said.

Malcolm nodded.

"We should meet again. Here at seven o'clock tonight," Phil said.

Malcolm opened his mouth as if he would protest.

"We'll need to know what we've discovered, won't we?" she argued.

Malcolm frowned but nodded. He turned to me. "Could you recognize the man who was runnin' away last night?"

"I only saw his silhouette."

"Would you be willin' to go with me to where Ian works? Get a look at him?"

"Sure. I'll ask Gran if I can go."

"I'll ring you."

We walked out into the hall together.

"Malcolm," called a male voice. A tall man with a suitcase stood at the entrance of the B&B. He came and wrapped his arms around Malcolm in a big hug. "Laddie, I did no expect to find you here, but good to see you, all the same. I trust the family is well and prosperin'. Tell Jock I'll ring him tonight. I'd like to come by whilst I'm here." The man smiled and then scanned the room. "Do you know where I may find the innkeeper?"

I pointed to the kitchen door.

"Who's he?" Phil whispered.

Malcolm gave her a sidelong glance. "My father's cousin from Aberdeen. And there's no feud."

CHAPTER 28

Saturday, Continued!!!

Busy doesn't half describe the B&B that day. The police came. They took a statement from Mags and took away the knife. And the phone rang constantly.

Malcolm called. He wanted to meet me on Bruntsfield at 2:00. From Bruntsfield, Malcolm and I could go on the bus to the bakery where Ian worked. Gran said it was all right. I could go as long as I promised to only look at the man. I was not to say anything at the time. If Ian did resemble the silhouette I had seen last night, then Malcolm and I were to return to the MacLeod's bakery immediately and inform Mr. MacLeod. He would contact the police. I was to do nothing more.

Ian was turning into a real suspect. Malcolm had learned Ian didn't start work until 5 AM. So he could have been the one in the bakery and the one who slashed the tires.

Phil called. She said she had brilliant news, but she was not going to tell me until the meeting. Then she told me. Violet, the dress store owner, had a boyfriend who was an auto mechanic. (How did Phil find out that? Maybe she should consider becoming a reporter.)

"Promising info," Phil said. "But the walls in her shop show no sign of a door into the bakery. Not promisin'."

We decided that Violet should be moved down on the list of suspects.

Nunzio, the baker, called after lunch. It gave me the chills. I had just finished talking with Phil on the phone in the kitchen and was passing the hall phone on my way back up to Alejandra and room six, when the hall phone rang. It was Nunzio. My stomach lurched and the hairs on my arms stood up when I heard his voice. He wanted to speak to the Browns. I eavesdropped while pretending to dust the hall banister. He invited the Browns to dinner that night. The man was definitely moving up on the list.

By the time I got back to room six poor Alejandra had already changed both beds by herself and was starting on the bathroom. I felt bad. She was not getting much work out of me that day with all my running for the phone. While she worked on the tub and the toilet, I wiped down the mirror and cleaned the sink. Then I dusted the dresser tops extra quickly and the light bulbs. Room six was getting an "A" cleaning. (An "A" cleaning was required when the room was getting new guests. According to Gran, the guests would be arriving any moment.) Alejandra had just plugged in the vacuum when a cell phone went off. She jumped and her eyes searched the room. "*Chica,* do you see my ...?" Her hands patted her shoulders.

"Sweater?" I offered.

"*Si!*" She nodded. "Ah ... I remember." She went into the bathroom, took her sweater from the robe hook and fished a cell phone out of the pocket. She turned away. In a nanosec, she shot a look back over her shoulder at me. "Ah ..." She bit her lip. "*Mi madre,* my mother, she's ill. She wants me to call."

"But—" I stopped and jerked a nod. I ran the dust cloth again over the non-dusty bureau top, trying not to look her way as she closed the bathroom door. Alejandra had told Gran her mother was dead. I had heard Gran tell Aunt Susannah that's why Alejandra wanted the job so badly.

I crept to the bathroom door and put my ear to the crack. I couldn't hear what Alejandra was saying.

Suddenly she shouted something in Spanish. It jolted me. She was swearing. And I knew what she was saying. (A girl I had been e-mailing when I thought I was moving with my parents to Ecuador had written the exact words. She said using them would impress my new teachers. Fortunately, one of my teachers at my school in California spoke Spanish and clued me in.)

That Alejandra would swear didn't shock me. What jolted me was that the phrase was THE PHRASE I had heard the night before.

My mind reeled at warp speed. I saw myself sitting on Gran's steps a couple of days ago. I was petting Sunshine. Alejandra came through the gate. In her hands she had boxes of bakery cookies. She had THOSE cookies—the awful,

awful ones. Did she—? I gripped the doorknob. Alejandra had been ahead of me on Bruntsfield, but she got to Gran's after me. Why? She must have—

I stepped away from the door, wondering what to do next. In the movies the detective always confronts the villain. I hardly had enough spit to swallow. Saying anything to Alejandra was WAY not possible. I felt so angry and so confused. She had been nice to me when I cleaned rooms with her this week, really nice. Could she really be one of the bad guys?

I went to the vacuum cleaner and turned it on. Alejandra came out of the bathroom. She dropped her eyes, and coming to me, took the vacuum's handle. "*Mi madre,*" she said, still not looking at me, "she is worse. We must finish the room rapidly. I must leave."

I nodded, stepping away. I watched her, feeling hurt. She had lied to me again. I didn't want to be in the same room with her.

"I'll get the fresh towels," I yelled and bolted.

Aunt Susannah was at the linen closet. She put an arm across my shoulder.

I thought about telling her what I knew, but then it occurred to me I really didn't know a lot. There could be all kinds of reasons why Alejandra had lied and lots of people knew how to swear in Spanish. Lots. And so what if she was the one who had brought bad cookies from the bakery? I was reaching for the clean towels when I heard the slap-slap of someone's sandals. I turned. It was Alejandra.

"Miss Stewart, we are finished with the room, so I will leave now? I have an emergency—my family."

"An emergency, I'm sorry. Aye, if you need to leave now, we can manage the rest. However, Mrs. Stewart would like a word with you about tomorrow," Aunt Susannah said.

"Tomorrow?" Alejandra nodded and went downstairs.

I grabbed the towels and running, placed them in the room six. Then taking the stairs two at a time, I flew up to my room, pulled my jean jacket off its hook, and scooped some money out of the nightstand drawer. The gate clanged on the street below. Leaning way out the window, I saw Alejandra almost running down the street. I tore from the room. Someone needed to follow her.

I expected her to go up to Bruntsfield and meet her accomplice, maybe near the bakery. She didn't. She turned onto a side street and went to the door of an apartment building. She didn't buzz; she used a key. What was going on? She had told me she lived across town.

After she went inside, I raced to the door and checked the names next to the buzzers. Her name wasn't there. But obviously, she was good friends with someone who lived there—maybe her accomplice? I wished Phil was with me. Phil would have known if someone in the building was connected to the bakery.

Then it hit me. I could write down the names and show them to Phil. I could write them down—that is if I had a pencil and paper.

In the gutter were a paper bag and a business card. My skin crawled. Gritting my teeth (and telling myself I could wash my hands later with a lot, a lot of soap and water), I picked them up.

An older woman wearing an apron and carrying a broom came out of the apartment building next door.

"Please, would you have a pen or a pencil that I could borrow?" I asked.

Her forehead wrinkled. "You're an American, are you not?"

"Yes, ma'am."

"From where in America?"

"California."

"California, is it? I've heard it's a lovely place."

I forced a smile. Minutes were ticking away. I shot a look at the windows in the apartment building. My palms sweated. What if Alejandra glanced out the window? What if she came down and found me here?

"What would you be wantin' the pencil for, dear?" the woman asked.

"I-I--" A lie popped into my head. I could say I wanted it to draw a picture of a flower in her garden. I didn't want to lie. "Please, I only need it for a few minutes. I promise I'll give it right back."

The woman eyed me closely. She shrugged and went back into her building.

I grabbed the paper. The woman returned with a pencil. "Thank you, I'll bring it right back." I walked slowly toward the apartment building Alejandra had entered. The woman was watching me. I could feel it. I swallowed. What would she do when she saw me writing down the names?

from My Edinburgh Files

But a phone rang inside her building and she disappeared. Quickly I wrote down the names and then put the pencil on her doorstep. I checked my watch—2:00. Malcolm would be waiting for me. I ran to the corner. From there I could signal Malcolm on Bruntsfield and still watch for Alejandra.

CHAPTER 29

Saturday, 2:04

"Could be," Malcolm said, squinting at the tall, white building where Alejandra still was.

A puzzle piece suddenly fit. "Malcolm, nobody else complained to your father about bad cookies, right?"

"Correct."

"So the empire biscuits Gran got were switched. Maybe Alejandra did it there." I pointed to the apartment building.

Malcolm pushed the hair back from his eyes. "Hand me the list of names. I'll show it to people at the bakery and be back in two ticks."

"Malcolm," yelled a man coming up the hill. He raised a long, long arm in greeting. (I thought of a walking string bean.) The man looked me over and then gave Malcolm a crooked grin. "I knew the day was fast approachin' when we would be seein' you with a lassie. Pretty she is."

My face grew hot. Malcolm turned red. "Dennis, it's not that way, it's—" he said. Then he blinked hard and stared. "I thought you were gone to London, Dennis."

"Aye, I been and back. Two days, it took." He scowled. "Someone's been playin' a prank. And when I find out who it was, I will ..."

"Your mother's no ill then."

"No, mum's fine. She weren't even in London. She was up at m'sister's in York. Learn from me, laddie. A strange woman rings you in the middle of the night—you would be wise to ask a lot of questions."

"The phone call was from a woman?" I asked.

"Yes, said she was a friend. That should have tipped me. Mum's a fine person, but she doesn't take to foreigners."

"I don't understand," I said.

"The woman who rung me, she was a foreigner."

Malcolm looked past me, staring at the apartment building. "Dennis, I'll walk with you," he said as Dennis started up the block. "Please, Libby, wait here." He jerked his head at the building. Then he leaned over and whispered, "Stay hidden."

I ducked behind the hedge and hoped the people walking up or down the street would think I was playing hide-n-seek. Why had Alejandra gone into the apartment building? What was she doing in there?

I peeked around the edge of the bush. Suddenly the door of the apartment building opened. My breath caught in my throat. A man came out wheeling a bicycle. I inched away from the hedge to get a better look. I didn't recognize the man.

The door opened again. This time it was Alejandra. I jumped behind the hedge, frantically trying to figure out what I should do next. Should I stay or leave? If I stayed, what could I say to her when she found me standing here?

Pressing my face to a small break in the leaves, I watched Alejandra walk briskly to the sidewalk. But instead of coming toward me, she turned and walked the other way. At the corner she turned onto the street that Phil and I had run down the night of the trash fire. I followed her.

When she got to Bruntsfield, she crossed the street going toward the bakery. Yes! We had her. She would do something incriminating there and we would catch her at it. Yes! I ran, scared and excited at the same time.

After racing to the bakery door, I forced myself to walk in casually. I scanned the room. Malcolm and his father were standing in the back doorway, talking. Some customers, Americans, were peering into the cases, discussing what to buy. But no Alejandra. I tore across the room to Malcolm. "Alejandra, is she in the back?" I tried to whisper it.

"Who?" Mr. MacLeod asked. "Customers are no allowed in the work area."

Malcolm's head whipped around toward the work area, anyway. "No, she's not here."

Embarrassed, I pulled at my hair. "Maybe she didn't come in." I backed out the door, still having a hard time believing that she wasn't there.

I went into the dress store. (I don't know how I got so brave.) I expected to find Alejandra and Ms. Murdock whispering. Ms. Murdock was alone. I checked the space below the dressing room curtain, no feet. Then I figured

Alejandra might have needed something copied. I looked in the window of Phil's mom's copy store. But again no Alejandra. Puzzled and defeated, I returned to the bakery.

"I lost her," I said to Malcolm.

Phil rapped on the window and came in. "What is it? What's goin' on? I saw you look in the copy shop."

I explained.

"No. We've not lost her. She's there." Phil said, pointing out the window. Partly hidden by a large woman in a black coat was a long black braid. The large woman stepped into the street. Now I saw her. Alejandra was at the bus stop.

I pushed at the door, but Malcolm grabbed my jacket and pulled me back. "If we walk out there and get on the bus, she might well think we're followin' her."

I sighed and tugged at my lower lip. He was right.

Phil's eyes narrowed and she cocked her head—she was thinking. Then she grinned mysteriously and ran out the door. In less than two minutes she was back. "Come on. The bus is here."

"But—" I started to protest.

"There's no time. Come on," she insisted.

Malcolm and I followed. Phil began chattering about something as if we were just three friends hanging together. What she talked about, I haven't a clue. I was too nervous to listen. I just kept walking and trying not to look at Alejandra.

At the bus stop Malcolm and I started to queue up. Phil grabbed my arm, pulling me away from the line. "Walk past it," she whispered. "And smile, act casual."

Out of the corner of my eye I watched Alejandra getting on the bus. We were going to miss it and lose her if we didn't get back in line now. I tried pulling my arm free.

"No, this way," Phil said, dragging me and Malcolm farther down the street. "Get in that cab." She pushed me toward the cab, a car's length behind the bus.

"What?" I protested.

"Get in," she said, opening the door.

We did.

"Terry," Phil said to the cab driver, "as they say in American films, follow that bus."

CHAPTER 30

Saturday, 2:45

Following the bus, the taxi rode past the park, known as the Bruntsfield Links, and down the wide street. I noticed the shops and cafes that I had seen on the day I got lost. That had been Wednesday. Incredible! So much had happened since then.

The bus and our taxi had to slow to a crawl as the street filled with cars and buses. The sidewalks, I noticed, also had become more crowded. I leaned forward and looked across Terry's shoulder. We were coming to a place where the road split into a big Y.

"What is this place?" I asked.

"This is Tollcross," said Terry, sounding like a tour guide. "In medieval times people coming into the city on market day with their goods paid the toll here.

The mention of money made me root around in my pocket. I pulled out two brass pieces—pounds—and some silvery coins. Was it enough?

The bus turned up the right arm of the Y and stopped. The back door of the bus opened and we held our breaths. Alejandra did not get off. The bus roared again and climbed the hill.

"How much farther is she going?" I asked, hoping I had enough money to pay for our ride.

"We're comin' up on the Royal Infirmary," Phil said.

"Uh?"

"The hospital," Malcolm explained.

"Oh, no," I groaned. "This is just a wild goose chase. Her mother really is sick."

The bus came to a stop. I chewed my lip, my eyes glued to the bus. A tall, thin man got off. A woman with a small child followed. Alejandra didn't get off. The bus coughed and moved on. I sighed and flashed a grin at Malcolm. He didn't seem to notice. Instead he leaned forward, and stared straight ahead, his eyes glazed as if he were looking at something beyond the bus.

As the bus rounded a busy corner, Malcolm's head slowly turned to the opposite corner and then swung back to the bus. The bus continued a few yards and then stopped. Malcolm scrambled across Phil and stared out the window.

"What's happening? What do you see?" I asked.

"Nothing. I see nothing. Except the back of a large head," Phil grumbled.

"Passengers are disembarking from the bus," Terry offered.

The bus pulled away. Phil gasped and Malcolm's head sunk into his shoulders. "Nunzio's," he muttered angrily.

I craned my neck to get a better look at the crowd. Standing at the curb, trying to get across the street, was Alejandra.

"Duck," he ordered, and turning around, he pushed my head down below the level of the window.

The taxi inched forward.

"Let us off, please, as soon as you can, Terry. But nearer the entrance to Greyfriars," Malcolm said.

The taxi picked up speed and rounded the curve in the road. Malcolm jerked up and clambered to the back window. "She's goin' into a restaurant on the other side of the street. Please, can you stop?"

Terry pulled over to the curb. Malcolm shot out of the taxi and ran toward the street. I opened my hand with the coins in them. Phil dropped in a few more silvery pieces and jumped out the door.

"Is that enough?" I asked Terry.

He started to shake his head, but then he stopped and shrugged instead. "Aye, luv, it's fine. Be careful now." He grinned.

I nodded politely and scrambled out of the taxi. Terry had been kind. The money wasn't enough—I could tell. I was grateful for his kindness, but he thought we were just playing a game.

We weren't.

Phil and Malcolm were already across the street. When I reached them, they were arguing fiercely about who should go into the restaurant. We couldn't all go. It would be way too suspicious. But one of us had to go in and see who Alejandra was meeting. (That's what we decided she was doing there—meeting someone.)

Phil won out. She said she could go in and use the loo (the restroom). The restaurant owner would be more likely to let a girl than a boy.

"What are you going to do if Alejandra notices you?" I asked.

"She'll notice me because I'm goin' to notice her. I'll say, 'Don't you work at Mrs. Stewart's B&B?' If you do not act as if you're sneakin' around, people will no think you are."

"Come on," Malcolm said to me, "we'll wait and watch from the greengrocer's." He pointed to a store across the street.

The greengrocer sold fruits and vegetables. He also sold ice cream bars—lollies, they're called. As we entered the store, we passed a refrigerator case of them. My mouth watered. Detective work was giving me an appetite.

While Malcolm watched from the window, I checked out the contents of the refrigerator case. Malcolm smiled and offered to buy. Unwrapping orange juice bars with cream centers, we again took up positions at the window. I was just licking into the cream part when Malcolm suddenly sighed. Across the street a heavy set man with graying hair and mustache was entering the restaurant. I recognized him.

"Nunzio," Malcolm mumbled.

"Do you think he is the saboteur?"

Malcolm looked pained. "I don't know. His shop is around the corner. He might be goin' into the cafe to eat," he said hopefully.

I knew how Malcolm felt. It was hard for me to imagine Alejandra being part of the scheme. She had seemed so nice.

Malcolm bit savagely into his ice cream bar. "Nunzio would no harm my father. He's a pal." A chunk of frozen orange juice broke loose and fell on the floor. For a moment Malcolm just stared at it sadly. Then grimly he scooped it up and tossed it into a wastebasket.

Phil dodged traffic and, panting, entered the shop. "You—you two are an advert standin' there. Everyone can see you. Come on," she ordered, leading us down the block and away from the restaurant. We came to an alley and she stopped, motioning us into it. "A short, heavyset, old guy just came in and sat down with Alejandra. They're at a table in the back corner. It's sure they're planning something."

"Are there other people in the restaurant? Other men, old as you say?" Malcolm asked.

"No."

"There must be." Malcolm looked angry, desperate. "Are you quite sure?"

"I am. Why the questions? The old guy with the mustache must be behind your father's troubles. Now all we need do is find out who he is and what is his connection."

"I need to get to my father's bakery." Malcolm turned and walked stiffly up the street.

"Wait," Phil cried, "we need to find out who the man is."

"We know who he is," I said quietly, sadly.

CHAPTER 31

Saturday, Continued

We had to walk back to Bruntsfield (no bus money). Halfway there God turned on the sprinklers. Cold, cold water dripped down my face and, slipping inside my collar, slid down my back. I shivered—totally miserable.

Phil and Malcolm didn't notice the rain. They were having a huge argument. It was Phil's fault. She wouldn't shut up. Malcolm was really hurting and she wouldn't stop pelting him with questions and her theories. And then when we got to my corner, she told Malcolm that she was going with him to tell his father about Nunzio. Malcolm said no way—MYOB. Phil got really mad but, surprisingly, backed off. But then putting her arm across my shoulder, she yelled after him, "Tell us about it at the meeting tonight."

I pushed the wet hair from my face and stared at her. I couldn't believe it. She was not getting it. It was over.

Mystery solved. It was none of our business anymore. "I'm cold. I need to go," was all I could think to say. And I left her on the corner.

At Gran's I went straight upstairs to my blow dryer. Oh, it felt so good. Then I went looking for Mags. But she was out. Crumb! I wanted to tell her about Nunzio. And about Alejandra.

Depressed and bored I hunkered down in front of the TV in Gran's living room, but that was more boring than boring. After only a little watching, I clicked it off, and not knowing what else to do, I went back upstairs. A British fashion magazine lay on Mags' bed. I tried reading it, but my eyes kept closing. Finally I gave in and curled up on my bed. When I woke up, the clock read 6:30. Staring at it I wondered why nobody had called me for dinner. I took the stairs two at a time.

The kitchen was empty. Going into the hallway, I heard someone tapping away on the computer in the office.

I pushed the office door open farther. "Hi."

Aunt Susannah stopped typing and turned. "Have a good lie-down?" she asked. "Splendid. You've had a busy week." Her eyebrows shot up playfully and she smiled. "Do you want to check your e-mail?"

I shook my head. "Later."

"Your grandmother's gone to an early music event. She considered waking you but decided sleep was preferable. That was fine with you, was it not? Though it puts me in mind. We've got to get you to one of the children's shows on the Festival Fringe whilst it's still on. They can be fantastic."

I frowned.

"Some of the shows are for very young children, but not all of them. Tomorrow we'll have a look at the program. There are a number of them on the table in the entry hall. You could have look tonight for yourself if you like. After dinner, I suspect." She grinned. "There's macaroni cheese and greens and tomato salad in the fridge for you. Pop the pasta in the microwave—three minutes."

I started to close the door.

"Oh, Elizabeth, please, before you take your supper, go 'round to Claire's? I've not been able to get through on the phone. Tell your sister I want her straight home."

"I thought Mags was on restriction and not allowed to be out at night?"

"She is, but apparently she has forgotten." She glared at the computer. I had a feeling my aunt's angry look wasn't about something on the screen.

At Claire's, her mother came to the door. She said—I couldn't believe it—Margaret WASN'T there.

"May I talk to Claire?"

The phone rang in another room and Mrs. Webster said quickly before shutting the door that Claire was not home, but she was expected.

"Wow, Mags, you are really in for it." I shook my head. Obviously Mags was out someplace with Claire. My sister was acting brain-dead. Why??? It wasn't like her.

I trekked back up the street. Ahead of me a dark-skinned girl with black hair was dribbling a soccer ball. The girl was about my age. Did she live on the block? I walked a little faster.

The girl kicked the ball too hard and it got away from her. It raced toward me. I wanted to kick it back, but wasn't sure the girl would like that. I scooped it up instead.

"Hi," the girl said, running up.

"Hi," I said back and handed her the ball.

"Roopa," a woman in an Indian sari called from the steps of a nearby house. "Come in, we are waiting supper for you."

"Straight away, Mum," the girl called. She shrugged and smiled at me. "Cheers," she said and ran toward the house.

"Yeah, cheers," I called after her. I kicked at a rock on the street. Why did she have to go in before we even got a chance to talk? I trudged back to the B&B.

Aunt Susannah came into the kitchen while I was eating my dessert—summer pudding. She slid her arms into a tan jean jacket and said she would be out for a couple of hours. She was meeting friends for dinner at a restaurant on Morningside. (I nodded my head like I knew where Morningside was, but I hadn't a clue.) We were not to worry. The guesthouse was full, so no new guests would be arriving and we—Mags and I—should let voice mail take any calls. "If you would like more than sisterly company, you may ring Pippa and invite her to spend the evening," she offered.

"No, thank you," I mumbled.

She nodded.

"Aunt Susannah, I saw a girl in the street playing soccer. She's about my age."

"Soccer? Oh, that would be Roopa. Lovely girl and quite clever." Aunt Susannah pulled at an earring and smiled as if to say, 'Would you like to meet her?'

Did she mean tonight? I looked away. Suddenly I felt, well, shy. And I worried that if I said I would like to meet her, Aunt Susannah would take me over to the girl's house and introduce me. That would be too weird, like a play-date for little kids. And what if Roopa didn't like me or I didn't like her? What would we do? No, I didn't want to meet anyone new. Not tonight.

Aunt Susannah seemed to trust me on this one. She said nothing for a moment. Then she asked, "Where's Margaret?"

"She's coming," I hedged as I took two more spoonfuls of cream and berries. I didn't think I was telling a lie. I thought it was the truth. I was sure she and Claire were on their way to Claire's and that any moment Mags would come bursting in. So why say anything and get Mags in any more trouble?

Bad! Bad, wrong, stupid decision!

CHAPTER 32

Saturday, 8:05

At 8:05 Mags had still not appeared. I stomped down to Claire's.

Claire answered the door, a cordless phone held to one ear. She held up one finger.

"Mags is going to be in major trouble," I blurted out. "She has to come home now."

Claire frowned. "Hold a minute," she said into the phone. "Margaret is not here," she said to me.

"Where is she?"

Claire shrugged. "Why would I know?"

"But she was with you."

"No."

"Your mother said when I was here a little while ago that both of you were out someplace together."

"My mother would not say that. She knew I was at harp practice and that I went alone."

"I'm confused," I said. My stomach flip-flopped—fear. "My aunt said Mags came down here."

"Yes, but that was this afternoon. Before she went out with Jamie."

I gasped. "She went out with Jamie! She's on restriction, she's not—"

"There's no need to get excited, little one. It wasn't a date. He come 'round and asked her to go with him on errands. She was concerned about gettin' back in time for her curfew. He said it would no be a problem." Claire smiled a sly smile. "It appears it was."

Claire's "attitude"—as my mother would have said— made me want to throw something at her. How could she be so cold about someone who was her friend? And how could my sister think going out with Jamie wasn't a date? "Do you know where they went?" I managed to ask.

Claire fluttered her eyelids. I took that for thinking. "The Balmoral—where the food fete will be tomorrow. And some bakery, I think."

Bakery?!! Nunzio's?!! The Nunzio who had had a knife last night?!! My stomach knotted. I tried to swallow. "It's OK. She was with Jamie," I mumbled, trying to reassure myself.

"Sorry? What?" Claire asked.

"Oh, nothing." Nothing? I hoped it was nothing. I hoped everything was—

I wanted to talk to my sister. I NEEDED to talk to my sister—to know that everything was all right. I stared at the phone balanced on Claire's shoulder. "Can I—may I please use your phone?"

Claire shook her head. "No way."

I decided I didn't care. Claire could just be annoyed with me. "Please, may I use your phone?"

She stared for a moment and then brought the phone to her ear. "I'll ring you back in a sec," she said and handed the phone to me.

Then the universe collapsed again. I didn't know the number. "Do you know the MacLeod's number?" I asked.

She rattled it off. My hand shook as I punched in the numbers.

A man answered.

"Hello, Mr. MacLeod, this is—"

"There is no MacLeod here," the man said.

"I'm sorry," I mumbled to the click. I couldn't even handle the phone! "God, please help," I prayed silently. "Wrong number," I said, biting my lip. "Could you tell me the number again?"

"Hand it here. I'll do it."

"No, please, I can, I want to—"

She told me the number and again I punched numbers in.

Malcolm answered.

"Malcolm!" I was so glad to hear his voice. "Malcolm, this is Libby. May I speak to my sister?"

"She's no here."

My stomach knotted again. "Um, well then is your brother home?"

"No, he's not here either."

She was STILL out with Jamie. What was she thinking? "Malcolm, if my sister comes to your flat, would you please tell her to call me at my grandmother's?"

Claire's mother called her from some other part of the house and Claire left, smiling a gossipy smile.

"Malcolm, Claire said they were doing errands. She said they went to a bakery? Did she mean Nunzio's?"

Malcolm was silent. It felt like an hour. Then he spoke slowly. "I don't know. I told my brother what we had discovered. He might have decided to fetch our extra key."

"He didn't tell you when he got back to your father's shop?"

"I was already to home. I didn't see him or Margaret. Is there something wrong?"

The whole scene at the airport, the whole embarrassing, awful scene, with my thinking Mags had been kidnapped flashed through my mind. "Probably not, no. Thanks for your help. Good night."

I could hear Claire and her mother. They were having what my mother calls a "discussion," so I put the phone on the table and left.

In the B&B's office I checked voice mail to see if Mags had called. She hadn't. Jamie had though—twice.

"Margaret, this is Jamie. I've got your jacket. You left it in the van. Luv, I waited for you at the Balmoral as long as I could. I hope you understand."

"Margaret, Jamie again. I'm still doin' for m'dad. Ring me on the mobile, luv. I want to know you got home safe. I'm thinkin' I should not have left you at Nunzio's."

The panic rose. Mags was NOT with Jamie. He left her at Nunzio's. Why? And WHY didn't she show up at the Balmoral? She met a friend, maybe. She was all right, I kept telling myself. No worries. Mags would walk in the door any moment.

I went out into the hallway to wait for her. I sat on the stairs. But that made me nervous.

The more I told myself not to be afraid, the more I didn't believe it. I started straightening up the papers beside the house phone—just for something to do. On the edge of a map of Edinburgh I saw a phone number. Mr. Brown had written it there when Nunzio had invited them to dinner.

The Browns! They had been coming down the stairs when I was going up to my room after giving up on TV. That was about five o'clock. They were going to Nunzio's bakery. I had heard them talking about it. Maybe Mags was at Nunzio's when they were there. I punched in Nunzio's number. A woman answered. It wasn't Alejandra.

"Are Mr. and Mrs. Brown still there?"

"No, they are gone. Who is calling, please? Is there some trouble?"

"Uh, I'm Libby. My grandmother runs the B&B where the Browns are staying."

"Oh, they are with my husband at our bakery. You may still be able to reach them there. Do you need the number?"

I wrote it down, thanked her, and hung up. I started punching in the numbers then stopped, trying to slow my mind, trying to think it through. If I called the bakery, I could talk to the Browns. But if I WENT to the bakery, I could also look around. Maybe I'd see things—get more clues about where Mags was. I needed to GO to the bakery.

My stomach lurched. I felt cold and hot at the same time. Would I be able to find my way to The Bread Shop? And if I got there, what about Nunzio? I shivered. I decided to push him out my mind. I would think about the Browns. They would be there. It would be all right.

I ran upstairs and scooped out all the coins from the drawer of the bedside table. Frustrated—I just held them in my hand. They wouldn't be enough for a cab, judging from Terry's reaction that afternoon. I felt sick—I would have to take the bus.

"You can do this. You can do this. But what bus—?"

I grabbed my jean jacket and went down to the office and called Phil. (OK. I admit it. After she had told me which bus to take, I was going to ask her to go with me.)

I got voice mail.

"Phil. I need help. I hope you get this message soon." I sighed. "If you come back in the next few minutes, call me. Please! I need to know what bus we took. No, I mean, what bus Alejandra took this afternoon. Call me back right away."

I drummed my fingers on the table. I paced the floor. Nobody called. I called Malcolm. No answer. I gave up and left.

The street lamps had popped on and the shadows around the trees beside the Goliath-tall wall were already black. It would be dark in a little while and not small-town-summer-night-friendly dark. I shoved open the gate anyway and ran down the street and up the hill. I ran until I got a side ache. It was only then I slowed down.

At the bus stop there were ten numbers listed on the sign. A bus came to the curb, the door opened. I stepped up to the bus. "Yes, luv," the driver said kindly, "where do you wish to go?"

"I-I-." Think, I told myself. "Do you know a bakery called The Bread Shop?"

He shook his head and reached for the door control.

"Wait, please. Do-do you go through—what's it called—tollbooth?"

He frowned, puzzled. "Would you mean Tollcross?"

"Yes, aye, and then go past the hospital?"

"Hop on," he said.

"I have this." I showed him the heavy brass coin.

"That's a pound," he said, "but never mind. Put it in, take a ticket and have a seat."

"Thank you." Tears came to my eyes. He was so nice.

I watched out the window for some familiar sights, recognized one building, but didn't recognize the next. Then I remembered the next and the next, but not the one after that. I got wet patches under my arms and I could smell my own sweat. Yuck! We came to Tollcross and I held my breath. The bus made the turn. It climbed the hill just as it had this afternoon. Whew! I was on the right bus!

As the bus came over the top of the hill, it pulled to the curb.

"Dear," said an elderly lady at the end of the bench seat, "this is your stop—Royal Infirmary. Hospital?"

"Oh, yes, thank you." I decided to get off and walk the block to the bakery. It was easier than explaining.

CHAPTER 33

Saturday, 8:45

Nearing The Bread Shop, I scanned the street. Major shock! A small black car was parked in front of the bakery, but the Brown's blue rental was nowhere to be seen. What should I do now?

The bakery was dark except for a window-square of light at the back of the shop. Beyond that hole in the wall was a room. I could make out a calendar and some cupboards. Suddenly Nunzio appeared in that room. I ducked down.

Fear wanted to freeze me to the spot, but something else, something so out of control that it scared me, was also building in me—fire-breathing anger. I wanted to pound on the bakery door and, when Nunzio answered, make him tell me where my sister was. This man knew. I was sure of it. I would make him tell me, somehow. I looked down at my hands. They had knotted into fists—small fists. Who

173

was I kidding? Why should he tell me? And what could I do if he didn't? "Oh, God," I prayed, "please help."

"Hey," whispered a voice behind me.

I nearly leaped out of my skin. But it wasn't God. It was Phil. "Phil!" I shrieked.

"Sh-h-h," she said, pulling me into the doorway of the charity shop next door. "I heard your message when I got home. I deduced that you would be here when I didn't get an answer at the B&B. Good detecting work, right?"

I nodded impatiently. "Mags is missing."

"You think she's here?"

"I don't know." I shuddered. Phil's question made me realize how much I didn't know. "She came here with Jamie in the afternoon. She didn't leave with him and she didn't meet Jamie later."

"Then we bang on Nunzio's door and demand he tell us everything. If he lies to us, we'll know. Then because we're suspicious of him, he'll lead us to her when we follow him."

"There's a step missing."

"What?"

"I don't know."

"It works."

"Where? In the movies? Phil, this is real life. And this is MY sister. Not some character in a play. What if after we ask him the questions, he decides to pick up the phone and tell whoever has got Mags to—well, I don't know—harm her?"

Phil bit her lip. After a moment she said more quietly, "What do you want to do?"

I shook my head and leaned back against the wall. What could we do? My mind was like an erased blackboard. I closed my eyes. It seemed so hopeless. "God, please ..." I whispered. I began to have an idea. "Is there a phone around here?"

Phil grinned and pulled a cell phone from her backpack. "Ta-da. My mother's. She left it by the house phone. I thought maybe—"

I took the cell and punched in the numbers. "Malcolm, this is Libby. Is Jamie there? I need to talk to him about Mags."

"She's no turned up?"

"No." I heard Malcolm repeat it all to Jamie.

"Libby, is it? This is Jamie. Your sister lost her watch. She thought at Nunzio's bakery. She left me to search for it there. But she's no turned up?"

"No. I'm outside Nunzio's bakery now. I thought I should ask him." In the background I heard Mr. MacLeod say, "Tell her to stay. I'll come."

"Did you hear that?" Jamie asked.

"Yes."

"Good." He hung up.

I thought it might be good, hoped it might be good. But how could I wait? It would seem like forever. I said a prayer.

CHAPTER 34

Saturday, 9:17

Finally a brown station wagon with MacLeod's written on the side pulled up.

Malcolm got out. He grinned sheepishly. "They'll be takin' away our detective license. We got it badly. Dad and Nunzio are workin' together. Nunzio intends to retire and sell m'dad his shop if we make a go of things at the fete tomorrow."

I slumped against the wall. We were at a dead end.

"Our most likely suspect turns out to be an ally," Phil said, stating the obvious.

"But then where is my sister?" I said angrily.

"M'dad has come to question Nunzio. Maybe he saw something." We turned at the approaching footsteps and followed Mr. MacLeod and Jamie to the bakery door. Mr.

MacLeod rapped on the glass and the light inside the shop came on. It took forever for Nunzio to open the door.

"*Buona sera, Buona sera.* Come in, please. Jock, how may I help you?"

Mr. MacLeod explained about Mags being missing.

Nunzio stroked his mustache. "Let me remember. Jamie, you come and want your father's key. You do not trust me, right? I see it in your eyes."

We hung our heads. This was so embarrassing.

"Eh, it's OK. We look through my office for it, right?" Nunzio walked to his office door. "It's not here. Then I remember that maybe it's in my special place for such things in the downstairs. I call down to Rory, but he doesn't hear me so I have to go down the stairs. The Browns, they are here with me, so, so we talk, we taste, they look 'round. Rory finds the key and brings it up to you, Jamie. Some minutes later I am leaving with the *Signor and Signora* Brown, and the young lady returns. She has lost some jewelry. I tell her it's OK, look in the office." Nunzio backed up into his office, as if he would look around, too.

Walking to the doorway, I made a quick survey of the desk and counters. I don't know what I hoped to find. Disappointed I dropped my eyes to the floor. Then I saw them. Mags' camel-colored shoes! I shrieked. Mags' flats were poking out from the space under the desk. I brushed past Nunzio and scooped them up.

"These are my sister's shoes. Where is she?" I demanded of Nunzio.

"Who was tendin' the shop when you left, Nunzio?" Mr. MacLeod asked.

"Only Rory. He was to close up."

"Where does he live?" I managed to ask.

"Da, come here will you?" Jamie called from someplace outside the office.

We found him on the stairs going down to the basement. He held out his hand. My body went cold as I stared at the gold object in it. It was my mother's watch.

I shrieked. "MAGS! MAGS! WHERE ARE YOU?"

From someplace in the basement came a banging sound. I shot down the stairs, the others running behind me. My mind reeling, I scanned the basement—large machines, cabinets, refrigerators. Where was the pounding coming from? Not this room. I spun around. Off to one side was a doorway to another room. Running into that room I spotted it—a shut wooden door. Someone was on the other side of it, pounding. As if I would twist it off, I turned the door handle and yanked. The door didn't budge. It was locked.

"MAGS?" I shouted and pounded on the door. "MAGS?"

"Libby? Is that you?" came Mags' voice from the other side of the door.

Nunzio used a key and my Mags fell out.

"Mags!" I cried, throwing my arms around my sister. "Mags!" I burst into tears.

Mags hugged me tight. "I'm so glad to see you. All of you. I thought no one would ever come! And I would never, ever get out of this closet. Well, I knew I would get out sometime. I figured with the fete tomorrow, one of the bakers would be here sometime tonight. But still I couldn't find the light switch, and when I did the light was out. And ugh, I kept picturing all kinds of creepy, crawly creatures around me." Mags shuddered.

"*Signorina,* my pantry is clean. No creepy creatures. But it is good we found you tonight. The fete tomorrow—I am not part of it. The next baker here would not be coming before Monday early."

"No." Horror swept across my sister's face and her knees buckled. Jamie caught her under the arm. "Thank you," she whispered, smiling up at him. Then she stared for a moment. Blinking, she jumped. "What time is it?"

"Nine thirty," Jamie said.

"We've got to leave. Alejandra and Rory, who works for you," she turned to Nunzio, "are planning to be at your bakery at nine thirty," she said to Mr. MacLeod. "I overheard them. They're the ones who have been sabotaging you."

"Da, the car keys," Jamie said. Mr. MacLeod handed him the keys and Jamie sprinted out of the room.

"But why would Rory ...?" Mr. MacLeod asked.

"Rory?" Nunzio asked, his voice full of disbelief.

Mags nodded. "Please, we have to leave now. I'll tell you on the way what I heard."

We hurried up the stairs and into the store part just as the MacLeod's station wagon roared up to the curb. All of us kids raced out the door and piled in. Nunzio and Mr. MacLeod ran for the small black car while Jamie pulled out into traffic. In only minutes the little black car passed us. Watching it slide in and out of lanes, I considered that

Nunzio was the kind of driver my mother doesn't like me to travel with.

As Jamie drove, Mags explained why she had come back to the bakery. When she went there with Jamie, she had noticed a folder and some paperwork in Nunzio's office. She left her watch hidden under some paperwork in Nunzio's office so she would have an excuse to return. She waited for Nunzio to leave and then asked Rory to search for the watch in the rest of the shop. She read the agreement between Mr. MacLeod and Nunzio, and then yelled, "Thanks," to Rory, who was in the back. She was about to leave the office when Alejandra came into the store. She remembered seeing Alejandra and Rory together at the museum. From Jamie she had heard that a foreign-sounding woman had sent one of Mr. Macleod's bakers on a wild goose chase. On a hunch she quickly hid under Nunzio's desk and then crawled to the doorway so that she could listen to their conversation.

"Alejandra and Rory had a terrible argument about tonight. Some of it was in Spanish, so I didn't get it all. Rory plans to get into the bakery and really mess things up. 'No! *Basta*,' she shouted at him. '*Basta*. We are going to get caught.' She said the police were involved and the kids, meaning us, were trying to find out what was going on. It was too risky. But Rory wouldn't listen."

"What are Rory and Alejandra planning to do tonight?" Phil asked.

"They didn't say."

The station wagon lurched as Jamie slammed on the brakes. A bus was pulling out in front of us. Traffic slowed to a snail's crawl.

"Can we no pull off onto a side street and go around?" Malcolm asked.

"Take longer," Jamie said.

Phil fidgeted. "This is makin' me crazy."

I agreed.

"Libby," Mags said, turning in her seat. "I thought about some things when I was locked in the closet. I had a lot of time. I mean, after I prayed, and—"

"The bus!" Phil shouted. "It's movin'."

"Aye, I see it," Jamie said, swinging the car around it and speeding up.

"Libby, please," Mags said, reaching for my hand. "I need to say this now. I've been kind of selfish lately. I—um—I've kind of shut you out. I'm so sorry."

I bit my lip. My eyes filled up. "Thanks, Mags." I said softly. "Thanks for saying it."

"How did you end up in the closet? They put you there, right?" Phil asked.

"No," Mags said. "That was my fault. When a customer came into the shop, I sneaked downstairs. That's when I must have lost the watch. I am so glad you found it, Jamie. I hid in the closet. I knew Rory would catch me if I stayed in the office. I thought I could sneak out after he left. I never thought he would lock the closet door."

Jamie shook his head. "From what Da says about Rory, I suspect he usually forgets."

CHAPTER 35

Saturday, 9:48

Nunzio's little black car was parked down a ways and across the street from the MacLeod's bakery. Amazingly there was an empty parking space behind the car. Jamie pulled into it as Mr. MacLeod was shutting the car door.

I shot a look at the bakery. There were no lights on in it. A shiver ran down my arms, and my stomach seemed to jump all by itself.

Mr. MacLeod ran back to us. "Open up," he demanded at the curbside door. Mags did and he reached in and snapped open the glove compartment. He brought out a flashlight. "Stop!" he ordered. "Get back in the car! All of you." He looked specifically at Malcolm and then the rest of us. "Nunzio, Jamie and I will go in first," he said, testing the light. "I no think Rory is dangerous, but I will not take the risk."

Malcolm opened his mouth, to protest I think, but quickly closed it again. He got back in the car and slumped against the seat. Mr. MacLeod nodded. Then dodging traffic, he followed Jamie and Nunzio across the street. Reluctantly, we closed the doors and locked them.

Phil, however, would not sit still. She fumed under her breath, and I noticed her hand didn't leave the door lock. Mr. MacLeod was only in the shop a few moments when I heard Phil unlock the car door and thrust it open.

"Stop her!" Malcolm ordered and then jumped across me. He grabbed hold of Phil's jacket. She tried to wriggle free. Suddenly she quit struggling and ducked down. "Alejandra," she stage whispered and pointed across the street.

I jerked around. Alejandra was down the block, near the corner. She was walking fast, almost running, toward the bakery and in her hand she was carrying something. The "something" had the shape of a plastic bottle. She stopped abruptly at the door to the bakery and looked into the window for what seemed like a long time.

"Let's grab her," Phil said.

"For lookin' in a window?" Malcolm snorted.

I gulped in a lot of air. I had been holding my breath and suddenly my body reminded me I needed to breathe. "What's she looking at? Do you think she sees your father and Jamie in the shop?"

"Dunno," Malcolm said.

"Why isn't she inside the shop?" I turned to Mags. "You said she and Rory were both sabotaging the bakery tonight. Do you think Rory isn't in there?" A jolt of fear flashed through me and my eyes darted up and down the street, searching for a man wearing a knitted hat.

"She's gone in," Phil said and took off across the street.

Malcolm, not waiting a nanosecond, ran after her. A speeding car nearly hit him. I stifled a scream. Mags threw open the door and scrambled out. I jumped out after her. Together we started into the street, trying not to get killed ourselves.

Unexpectedly Phil ran to the doorway of her mother's shop. Malcolm followed her and they disappeared into its shadows. Within seconds Phil reappeared and, crouching below the window, scudded for the bakery door. She was halfway there when Mags and I caught up with her.

"What about Rory? Maybe he's on his way here? We should stay outside and keep watch," my sister whispered, taking hold of Phil's arm.

Phil jerked free and continued her dash for the bakery door. Keeping low, we all ran after her. I reached her just as she was trying the door handle. The door was locked. She opened her mouth and immediately I clapped my hand over it. I think she would have bitten me, but Malcolm dangled a key in front of our eyes.

"I knew you would have that," she whispered scooting out of his way.

With his fingers, Malcolm searched for the keyhole and then silently used the key. It made only the tiniest of clicks. He turned to Phil and whispered, "Pippa, you have the mobile. Go to the doorway of your mother's shop, and if Rory appears, ring us on the bakery phone."

Phil frowned but went. Malcolm pushed open the door and the stupid bell tinkled.

I expected to hear running footsteps. Nothing. We stood like statues, waiting. But nothing. I stared into the shop's blackness, hoping—and terrified—to see something move. Everything was still. Shafts of light from the streetlamp outside lay dead on the floor and on the shelves. We crept past a case to the work area.

Suddenly something crashed on my left and someone pushed past me. I swiped the air, grabbing for anything. My hand found a thick rope of hair and hung on.

A blood-curdling scream pierced the air. "Ow-w-w! *Mi lastimasti!* My hair, let go!" Alejandra shrieked. She thrashed about, swinging her fists. Suddenly she connected with my shoulder. Whoa! It hurt. I lost my balance and fell. But I held on to her hair. Alejandra fell on top of me. I couldn't breathe.

"Get off my sister! Get off her!" Mags shouted. She tried pulling Alejandra off me, but the woman was solid.

Then Alejandra screamed again as Mags rolled her over. I let go of Alejandra's hair and scooted away so I could breathe again.

In the basement below there were shouts. Then someone was running up the stairs.

"Stop him! Grab him!" yelled Nunzio. There was the sound of scuffling. More running footsteps on the stairs.

"Awk, no, what is it?" Malcolm shouted.

Something metal clattered to the floor. A man shrieked, and a large body hit the floor. Others were running up the stairs. The lights jumped on in the store. Rory was sprawled on the floor in front of the stairs. He crawled, trying to scramble to his feet in a pool of white goo. A can, the size of a bucket, and the source of the white stuff lay on its side near him. He got to his feet, his hands and trousers covered with the sticky goo. For a moment he stared, looking bewildered at us and the goo.

"Libby, do something!" Phil cried, standing in the doorway. In one hand she was holding up the cell phone. Obviously she had thought of something to do.

All I could think of was to stick out my large feet in hopes of tripping Rory.

There was no need. Malcolm, his face slathered with the dripping goo and looking like some creature in a horror film, lunged for Rory. Rory pushed him off. But in doing that he stumbled over the can and went down again.

Outside the sirens whooped, getting louder and closer. Suddenly Alejandra broke free from Mags and, slamming Phil back from the door, tore out of the shop.

Blue flashing lights bounced on the wall opposite me. The police were here. I looked over at Rory spread out in the goo. Nunzio was sitting on top of him. At least we had one of them.

—*from My Edinburgh Files*

CHAPTER 36

Saturday, 9:57

There was a knock on the glass of the open bakery door. Mr. MacLeod nodded to the police officer standing there and the officer entered. Behind him was a policewoman. She was escorting Alejandra.

"PC Keith," the officer said, identifying himself and closing the door. "The station received a call."

"I made the call," Phil said, holding up the cell phone.

"I'm Jock MacLeod," Mr. MacLeod said to the officers. "And this is my shop. This man," he pointed to Rory, "and this woman broke in."

"We had a key," argued Rory. "We did no break in." Nunzio, who was standing over him like a fat eagle, glared. Rory looked at the floor. It seemed to me, he didn't dare to stand up. I think he didn't want to face his boss or Mr. MacLeod. I didn't blame him.

187

"Did you have permission to use the key?" the officer asked.

Rory chewed his cheek and dropped his gaze sullenly to the floor.

"I am cautioning you," PC Keith said, "that whatever you say can be used against you."

"We, Nunzio and I, came into my dark shop and found Rory hiding downstairs. Nunzio tried to stop him from getting away. But Rory ran past him," Mr. MacLeod said.

"I met him at the top of the stairs," Malcolm said. "He threw icing in my face."

PC Keith took out a notebook and pen. "I will be needing a statement from each of you as to what has occurred here tonight. PC Fleming, call for backup."

Nunzio put his finger into the icing dripping from Malcolm's cheek. "Jock, what do you put in your icing. A little amaretto, *si*? Oh, you are not going to say. Never mind. *E buonissimo! ottimo!* And you," he turned to Rory, "why were you making off with the bucket?"

"I was not stealin' it. I forgot I was carryin' it."

"You forget. Always you forget what you are doing. I tell him always it will get him in trouble. He needs to think about what he is doing."

"Why did you do this, Rory? I consider you a pal," Mr. MacLeod said not without kindness.

Rory shrugged. "I wanted to buy The Bread Shop from Nunzio. I've been savin' and some acquaintances are interested in partnerin' with me. But I do not yet have enough money, and the partners have no come 'cross with theirs. I said somethin' to—" Rory indicated Nunzio. "But he gave me not the time o' day when I talked about it. I knew that if you did well at the fete tomorrow, you would buy Nunzio's shop. If you didn't do well, you would have to wait, and by then, I would have the money. I was no tryin' to ruin you, Jock. Only tryin' to slow things down a bit. I am your friend."

Mr. MacLeod sighed deeply and looked sad.

"Some pal," Jamie said, scowling. "You steal my knife and then slash tires with it so that all the world thinks that I am the culprit. What do say about that?"

"I lost my head. But I did no steal the knife. I found it on the sidewalk the day you and your dad were goin' at it out front."

PC Keith cuffed both Rory and Alejandra and led them away.

CHAPTER 37

Sunday Night :)

From: Libby Carlsen
Subject: More to tell
To: Tom Carlsen <tcarlsen@christiancom.net>

Tom,

WOW, have i got a lot to tell u! Even more than what i told u on the phone last night. Which reminds me, i forgot to tell u Phil found out why Alejandra had the plastic bottle. It was full of liquid soap. They were going to add it to the icing and then spread the icing on the empire biscuits. That icing is used on a lot of other bakery stuffs that Mr. MacLeod was taking to food fete too. Ugh, I'm sure glad we stopped that from happening.

Hey, we went to the fete today. And you should have seen the hotel—the Balmoral. It was FAB! Very posh. And the doorman wears a kilt.

Mr. MacLeod invited Phil, Mags, and me to come, since we helped solve the mystery. He got us in as his helpers. We served the "biscuits." It was cool. You should have seen people eating the millionaire shortbreads, the ones with the caramel. It got all over their teeth, but they didn't care. Neither did we. (Mr. MacLeod ordered us to eat some so we could honestly say they were grand. I love those kinds of orders.)

Mr. MacLeod also offered to take us all to the Royal Observatory. It is way on the other side of Edinburgh. They don't really use the telescope anymore. Big disappointment, but we can see the telescope.

And, and at church this morning, the pastor, when he heard that I love astronomy, said he had a friend, a grown-up, who is in an astronomy group. Pastor Macaulay said he would call Isobel and arrange a meeting. How's that for exciting? I could probably go up one night with the group and observe stars and planets with them.

And, AND I met another girl who goes to my new school. Her name is Roopa. I saw her at church and went right up and started talking to her—letting other Scots get to know my great and fabulous personality. Anyway, Roopa was born in India and lives two houses down from Gran. I didn't get to know her before because she's been on hols (holidays, vacation to you) with her family. She seems really, really nice, which is great because while i like Phil and she is definitely fun, i think maybe she could be trouble. But even if Roopa doesn't turn out to be friendship material, i start school on Tuesday. And well, I'm sure God has someone who will be a friend.

Mags is hanging over my shoulder reading this. She says she wants to make sure that what I say about her is accurate. Did u tell her what i said in my last e-mail?

Oh, Tom, guess what? (You'll never guess!!!) She just said i can (OK, I may) wear Mom's watch, and she is even going to talk to Mom about my being the keeper of it.

AND Mags just said, "I'm not going to call you *enfant* anymore. Because you're not. You are growing up."

Wow!! How's that?!!!! EM me soon.

Love, Libby :)

—from My Edinburgh Files

Your turn: WHAT DO YOU THINK?

I love a good story. I get caught up in it. Sometimes I even wonder what I would do if I were in the character's place. Do you?

1. Have you ever moved to a new town or gone to a new school? What did that feel like?

2. Read Psalm 1 and Proverbs 27:9. Do you think God cares about whether we make good friends or not?

3. What qualities do you want in a friend?

4. Have you ever decided to spend less time being around someone whom you used to spend a lot of time with? If so, why?

5. Libby decides that she will be friendly with Phil but not have her as her best friend. What do you think that will look like?

6. Phil says God is on vacation. What do you think she means? Have you ever felt that way? What does Hebrews 13:5 say?

7. What do you like or dislike about Mags? Do you think she acted in a helpful way toward Libby? In what ways are you helpful to younger children?

8. How do you think Libby is going to do in her new surroundings?

AUNT SUSANNAH'S SUMMER PUDDING
By Jill Neff and Nancy Ellen Hird

Ingredients

6 cups of summer fruit such as black currants.

(Black currants are readily available in Britain, but they are not in some parts of the United States. Other fruits that make a delicious pudding are a mix of strawberries and blueberries. Use four cups of strawberries and two cups of blueberries. You may also use raspberries or blackberries as part of the mix.)

A loaf of firmly textured white bread.

(Do not use pre-sliced white bread. The bread's texture is not firm enough and will fall apart.)

Butter for greasing the bowl

Heavy cream

½ cup of sugar

¼ cup of sugar for sweetening the cream

Directions

It is very easy to make a summer pudding. Butter the bottom and sides of a soufflé dish or other bowl (about 1.75 quart). Set aside.

Cut the loaf of bread into slices an inch thick, or a little less. Remove the crusts. Line the buttered bowl with slices of bread fitted close together.

Prepare the fruit by rinsing and draining it well. Hull the strawberries and cut them in half if they are large. Put the 6 cups of fruit in a large saucepan. Pour in ½ cup of sugar. Heat the fruit over medium heat, stirring until the fruit softens and sugar dissolves. Notice that juices are forming in the pan. It takes about 5 to 7 minutes. Remove the pan from the heat and allow it to cool slightly. Spoon the fruit into the breaded bowl, using a slotted spoon. Then with a solid spoon, spoon the juices over the fruit. Cover with a layer of bread.

Seal the bowl with plastic wrap. Place a saucer on top and weigh it down with cans of fruit or vegetables. Put the bowl in the refrigerator. Leave for 8 hours or overnight.

Remove the cans and saucer, take off the plastic wrap. With a knife or spatula, go around the edges of the pudding and loosen it from the sides of the bowl. Turn the pudding out on a large plate.

Whisk the cream (or you may whip it with an electric mixer if you like). Add ¼ cup of sugar toward the end for sweetening.

Dish up servings and spoon the sweet cream over the top.

Enjoy!

THANK YOU

There is a kind of myth that writers write their books all alone—it's just them, their computers, and God. And while writers do spend a lot of time writing with just God, He also does something wonderful. He brings other people into the process.

Many people have helped me with the writing of this novel. Some have supported me with prayer, some with constructive criticism, some with expertise, many with encouragement and kindness. (A few have done all of the above.) I want to thank them in print. Here is my list: Tom Hird, Jessica Hird, Jenna Freck, Sigrid Nielsen, Laure Paterson, Elena Freck, Donna Fujimoto, Ellen Graebe, Jennifer Rempel, Sheila Seifert, Pastor John Bruce, my sixth grade Sunday schoolers, Jerri Sue Newman, Pamela Walls, Laura Chellew, Linda Bertolami, Carol Green, SCUM (my writing group), the many young readers of my drafts (especially the Grijalva family, Caitlin Krack, Cassie Thompson, Jessica Chan, Taylor and Payton Johnson, Alana Fujimoto, Ashleigh Fong), Wilma Adamson, Brian Adamson, Graeme and Alison Keith, Sean McVey, the MacDonalds, Nathaela, Jill Neff, Pat Macauley, Jenny Krack, Jeannea Macauley, Janice Malloy, the Lothian and Borders Police and the kind, generous people of Edinburgh who listened and answered my tons of questions and allowed me to take tons of pictures. Thank you, thank you to you all.

Thank you also to the companies who so graciously responded to my request to use the names of their products.

I have this enormous fear that I've forgotten to name someone. I'm sure I have, but know that even if I have forgotten, God has not forgotten your efforts and your kindness to me.

Made in the USA
Charleston, SC
19 December 2016